WICKEDNESS AND FOLLY

stories

DONOVAN WHITLEY

LEFTOVER BOOKS | NEW YORK
2026

WICKEDNESS AND FOLLY

Copyright © 2026 by Donovan Whitley

All rights reserved. No part of this book may be reproduced or used in any manner without written permission of the copyright owner except for the use of quotations in a book review. For more information, address: booksleftover@gmail.com

First Edition
ISBN: 979-8-9926307-3-2

This is a creative work. Any similarities to persons living or dead is coincidence.

Cover Design: Anze Ban Virant
Interior Design: Adam Van Winkle

LEFTOVER Books
Born in Rochester, New York in 2021
Publishing books overlooked by the mainstream.
leftoverbooks.com

LEFTOVER
Books

PRAISE FOR Donovan Whitley and
WICKEDNESS AND FOLLY

"Whitley's characters make my skin itch, and his writing makes me worry. That's the mark of good noir. These stories floored me, then picked me up and slapped me awake. Keep an eye out."
- Anthony Neil Smith, author of *Yellow Medicine*

"A stark, unforgving force of nature that combines the best elements of noir and literature."
- Frank Bill, author of *Donnybrook* and *Back to the Dirt*

"The grit lit nephew of Larry Brown and William Gay ... To read *Wickedness and Folly* is to sidle up to the bar and listen to your favorite town drunks tell you their dirty jokes and folktales about a charismatic and rascally cast of delinquents, miscreant, and ne'er-do-wells doing what they need to do to survive life in the rotten parts of Middle America."
- BULL Magazine

"...Whitley has a knack for crafting gritty, sharp-edged scenes with clipped sentences that spike the tension and capture the frenetic, unstable characters on the fringes of society..."
- Kirkus Reviews

CONTENTS

Bear Trap
9

A Reasonable Amount of Trouble
21

Ouroboros
33

Water Through a Sieve
43

The Chainthrower
55

Company of Awful
73

Come Not Forth from the Dust
77

Ablutions
105

The Dark Woods
111

Acknowledgments
127

BEAR TRAP

I'd been arguing with my girlfriend when she left the living room, came back with my revolver, and fired all six shots at me while I sat on the sofa. Apparently, I had done something, said something, perhaps threatened. I really don't remember.

For a brief moment, I thought that I could feel actual bits of my skull powdered in my hair, but when I probed delicately about, I found, shockingly, that it was only clots of sheetrock that had exploded from the wall above my head. It made a perfect crescent. How had she missed? That's what I kept thinking about. She was standing right there, not five feet in front of me. I will never forget that.

I should have died many times in my life—I should have died that night, but Fortuna, for whatever reason, had spun her wheel sunward for me. But she wouldn't forever.

"You done?" I asked her. "Did you get it all out of your system?"

She said nothing, only threw the revolver at me, wept into her palms, and left. I remember loneliness crystallizing in my blood, crushing coldly through my veins.

After the fight, after junking the last of my heroin and staring at the bullet holes in the wall with a numb, buzzing mind, I got in my banged-up Toyota truck and limped the thing across town to The Bear Trap. It was a lousy, crumbling cinder block dungeon that harbored people like myself, and the dark passengers inside us.

The Bear Trap was musty and smelled of stale beer and cigarette smoke. There were a few midday drunks, a mail man and some Apache Indians chittering and laughing at the bar. I recognized a man I'd not seen in some time, and whom I'd been acquainted with at the Otero County jail when I was eighteen—a man named Freddy Ochoa, sitting alone at a table off toward the back, drinking vodka. One side of his face was bloated with a big purple bruise, a nasty bruise, and had several cuts mended with butterfly tape. A hospital discharge bracelet hung loose about his thin dark wrist. I ordered a beer and took a seat across from him. Freddy sipped his vodka. A little dribbled down his yellow nicotine-stained beard. "What happened to you?" he asked me, probably referring to the sheetrock still powdered in my hair, and the split lip from the airborne revolver that I hadn't even known hit me in the face until he added: "Did you kiss a table-saw?"

"I got in a fight with my girlfriend," I said. "You?"

"Ah, I got hit by a school bus."

A school bus, I thought. "Again?"

"Yeah. My lawyer says there's a good chance I won't get any settlement from it either. Something about tribal this, tribal that."

"Did he tell you why exactly?"

"Yep," he said, rotating the glass on the table. "Mostly because I was high."

"Oh," I said, with weak opiated breath.

We drank several more beers together. Over the course of the afternoon, he consoled to me, cried to me, begged me not to leave, promised me that if I assisted him with a little job that he'd send me on my way with a gift of heroin for my troubles. Besides, I was broke and knew as long as I had heroin, my girlfriend would give in.

"I need a first mate on a repo job," Freddy proposed.

"A what?"

"A crew hand—do I need a piece of paper and crayons to make it any more clear? I need a goddamned partner."

"Okay," I said. "All right. What kind of repo job?"

"Just a little old job," he said. "I've got the saw, but I need your lousy truck, and you're the only lousy ass mother here that has a vehicle."

We drove with the windows down. My bones began to ache. I was getting sicker; when I coughed, I coughed up hot embers from the universe of my sick soul. He had me take him up into the mountains, into the Mescalero Apache reservation. He gestured vaguely down a narrow road off the highway. What he led me to was a salvage yard of sorts deep in the high conifer forest.

"Park off over here," Freddy said discreetly, hunching to scan the country with his wild, rheumy eyes.

"What are we getting out of here? We're not stealing one of these pieces of shit, are we?"

Freddy leaned back between the seats, retrieved a reciprocating saw from the canvas tool bag he had on the seat and laid it crosswise upon his lap. "Fetch that pair of bolt cutters back there, would ya?"

Stomping through the tall weeds to the sagging cyclone fence, no word was spoken between the two of us. It was a good hard walk from the roadbed. The only thing beautiful about this moment was the cannonading sounds of birds calling forth in a benevolent din from the treetops. But even that quickly made me want to puke. In truth, all I wanted to do was lay in one of the dark corners of The Bear Trap and nod out. But I was on a mission. Huffing and sweating out of his swollen, antic face, Freddy said, "Somebody's already chopped through the fence."

"By God, isn't that perfect. Isn't that dandy."

So we filed through the fissure in the links. The first rotted hulk of a car we walked to, Freddy dropped to his knees and looked underneath it. "Whoo-we," he said, "Dumb sons of bitches missed this one, the very first one.

What are the odds, old buddy?"

"I don't even know what the fuck we're looking for. I thought you said this was a repo job."

Freddy pressed the little button on the battery of his saw, checking the charge, and said, "Keep a lookout. I've got to get to work."

"Okay," I said. "Sure thing." I stepped a couple of paces and sat on a rusted bumper while Freddy commenced to his work. There ensued an awful metal on metal sound from underneath the car. Catalytic converters was what we were after. He'd intended on selling them for scrap so we could buy heroin with it.

An hour later, Freddy had a pile of about ten catalytic converters when, of course, the car turned around the bend and labored up the grade to the gate in a fine spray of dust. "Shit shit shit shit," Freddy hissed. "That's my brother." He was scrambling on hands and knees like a panic-stricken infant.

"Your brother?" I asked. "What the fuck?"

"Go up and talk to him. Tell him—tell him I'm out at the moment. Tell him I went up to Ruidoso for lunch, or something."

I spat through my teeth. "So I work here?"

"Yes," Freddy said, watching this visitor at the gate from behind the quarter panel of a car. "Tell him I just hired you."

I did. I walked up to the man, Freddy's alleged brother, and through our succinct discourse, would discover that indeed it was Freddy's brother. In fact, his brother owned this place, and Freddy was his only employee.

"Where'd he go?" the brother asked, I forget his name now.

"He said he went to Ruidoso."

"Ruidoso."

"Yes."

"For? What did he go up to Ruidoso for? We've a body yard to operate."

"For lunch."

"It's two in the afternoon. And the gate's locked.

And who even are you? And where were y'all this morning?"

"He said something about thieves. Said I was too new to do much, so he locked the gate and went on his merry way."

"Well. Tribal police just came by my house looking for him."

"I'm not too impressed by him myself."

"Huh," the man said. He nodded perhaps only to himself and then reconnoitered the menhirs of dead automobiles, appliances.

"He's eating at the Hall of Flame, if you want to start hunting him," I said.

"How in the world did he make it to Ruidoso, anyway? He doesn't have a car."

"Hitchhiked."

The man flashed his obsidian eyes at me. "Dumb prick. Can't count on him for nothing."

He threw his hands up. "All right then. I will be back. I'll just drive down to the precinct."

"Can you unlock the gate before you go?" I asked.

In all we made a hundred dollars between three scrapyards. The day was dying now; the sun going down in a burst of flames like the wake of a comet, leaving behind a cool draft that rolled across my skin and under my shirt as we drove.

The guy he knew who had the heroin lived in a depressing clapboard house patched up in tarpaper somewhere on the reservation. It wasn't a far drive, but it was full dark by the time we got there, and I had a bad feeling in my gut.

Freddy had me pull into the dirt drive to the house. Weeds had overtaken the yard, grown up through the warped boards in the porch. The house got no light but for the cones of headlights. In the darkened picture window on the ground floor, a hulk of a figure parted the curtains slightly, moved them back. There were some ratty cars parked at random, some propped on cinder blocks, in the front yard. "Who's all in there?" I said.

"Freaky fucks," Freddy said.

When I cut the engine, we could hear muffled music coming from inside the house—blues. It sounded slow, kind of haunting.

We walked up a plywood sheet that covered the porch steps. I knocked on the door. Freddy warned me not to say much, and that it would only take a moment to get the heroin. "This guy is an absolute nut," Freddy told me, observing the house with his bad face. "Just follow my cues and we'll be good."

As soon as the door opened, Freddy elbowed my ribs, and we went in quickly. The colossal sized silhouette I had seen at the window emerged from a doorway immediately to our left. It was a woman who outweighed Freddy by about two-hundred pounds. She looked somewhat wrong. Not like she'd been born that way, but in a way such that important connections in her brain had been seared through and died. She didn't say anything. She just watched us. Freddy had me follow him through the trash of what room we were in—what once had perhaps been a living room—and through a doorway into a green-lit kitchen, where two men were at. One of the men sat on a ruined sofa by the refrigerator, torching a bowl wrapped in foil and hacking up his lungs. The other stood by the sliding glass door, leaning against a cabinet, eating an apple. "Who's this?" He threatened. This man was tall, dark, and had a long-plaited ponytail adorned with bones and turquoise stones. I had a feeling about him.

"He is straight," Freddy replied. "Get him a beer—you want a beer?"

"I'm okay, thanks," I said.

The ponytail studied me with an air of suspicion and said to the man on the couch, "David, turn the stereo down." And then immediately yelled, "Turn the stereo down!"

David jolted and fumbled the knob down on the stereo next to him. "You know," the ponytail said to Freddy. "If you'd have actually called me, I'd have strongly advised against bringing him here."

David whinnied like a horse, rocked slightly, and

torched the bowl again, coughing.

"What crawled up your ass? I said he's straight," said Freddy.

"He can't stay. I don't want him around here."

"He isn't. I'm just getting him some compensation for driving me all the way out here."

The man took a bite out of the apple, and said while chewing, "Compensation?"

"Jesus—some heroin," said Freddy. The ponytail then angrily told the woman to escort Freddy into the next darkened room, leaving me helpless, and far from God.

I didn't know what to say and remembered Freddy's warning about not talking much. The ponytail took another small bite from the apple and pointed at my feet with it. "Careful where you step," he said, chewing.

"Why?"

"Because you're standing on a pentagram, bonehead."

And he was right. Just below my shoe soles, where the linoleum had been carefully pried away, lie a huge pentagram drawn in black paint, and I was standing directly in the middle of it. To this day I believe, in my heart, that this ponytailed Indian had marked a curse on me, as events later in my life, not very much later, in fact, would predict. David was staring at me now like a somewhat backward pupil and drooling, his eyes drifting slowly apart from each other, as if his eyes were fearful of his nose.

The ponytail finished his apple and gracefully placed the core of it on a dirty countertop and said to me, wiping his hands on his shirt, "How'd you meet your little friend?"

"You mean you don't know him?"

"Of course not. I know he's a dope-head. I know that much."

Then, Freddy, after what had felt like an eternity, returned into the kitchen, the hulk of a woman waddling behind. Freddy stood at my elbow, and we watched while the big woman handed cash to the ponytail. "Very good," he said, slowly counting the money. "You're a good girl. A wonderful girl. The best girl."

We were turning to leave, the colossal woman acting as our escort once again when the ponytail said, "Hey now."

We stopped and swung our heads around like puppets.

The ponytail pursed his lips in a manner of frustration and recounted the money. I looked at Freddy, I could feel anxiety in my limbs like static electricity. Freddy just watched the ponytail. "Uh oh," the ponytail said. "Looks like we've got ourselves a little issue at hand here."

"And why is that?" Freddy asked coolly.

"I'm short here. I'm short here by about fifteen bucks."

"Count it again," said Freddy, shifting his weight.

"No. Huh uh. I've already counted it twice. You know what that would mean if I counted it more than that and expected a different result? It would mean I'm practicing insanity. And I'm not insane. So where's the fifteen bucks left on this balance?"

But Freddy kicked the knee of the big woman who in turn toppled over with a seismic inducing effect in the floor. Pictures rattled and fell from the walls. She lay clawing at her knee and squalling horrifically. I couldn't help but study this obscene instance until Freddy punched my shoulder and called for me to run. We bolted through the door and leapt from the porch into the grass and ran full tilt across the yard and to my truck.

I was fumbling for my keys when Freddy said, "Here he comes, that psycho mother." I glanced at a perfectly black shape sprinting through the dark. A demon. That's who that man was. I stuck the key into the ignition and fired up the truck. But putting it into gear, I heard what sounded like a buckling of metal somewhere in the back. The ponytail had jumped into the bed of the truck and was now fetching kicks at the rear window. "Lose his ass!" Freddy yelled. "Lose him!" I gunned it, but the ponytail didn't give up. Swinging and swerving the truck along the gravel road, the kicks came just the same. It was as if this demon had defied simple laws, or perhaps the equipoise of earth had altered. Whatever it was, he simply would not give up.

The rear window finally broke open and peppered us with bits of stinging glass. A dark hand slipped through, clasping about at random like someone trying to catch flies. Freddy leaned back and bit the ponytail on the finger. No scream reported back though. I really goosed it now. We rocketed up a hill. I stood on the brakes and cranked the wheel way to the left, the ass end of the truck swinging hard to the right, kicking up loose gravel under the tires like rope unreeling from a spool, pinging and singing off of the wheelwells. The ponytail, launching from the bed of the truck, sailed headfirst into the trunk of a tree. Through the red haze of the taillights in the spurs of dust, the ponytail lay absolutely still on his back, like a sleeping acolyte.

Back at The Bear Trap all the people were dwarves. We walked in like kings. Despite the encounter with the Indian and his goons, that day was shaping up to be one of the best days of my entire life. I had actually worked for something. I'd sliced my hand somewhere along the way when Freddy had me work the saw, but it was all right. That's what happens to men who worked.

We'd only been in the place for five minutes when Freddy had elected, in his mind, to accuse the biggest, baldest biker guy in the room of cheating him out of a quarter during a game of eight-ball. With a pocket full of heroin and a brain full of beer, Freddy was feeling pretty brave. The biker stood down from the bar and blocked the fluorescent tubes overhead like some enormous movie monster. Freddy was scarcely up to the man's chest.

"Let's take it out to the back," the biker said.

"No," Freddy said. "Let's you and me be men. Let's fight right here. Right here in this room."

The Bear Trap had assumed a silence such that could be heard in a camp the night before battle. People had laid down their cards, stood off from the pool tables, the pinball machines, to watch this developing spectacle. I too was certainly interested in how this would play out.

But it had all built into a dud. The biker simply

laughed, called Freddy a dumb little drunk, and left. Things resumed as before; balls clacked across the felt, chatter swept up along the place. The engine of The Bear Trap was lubricated again. Freddy came walking back to me with a wide, yellow grin. His face shining, yet miserable. Some years from now Freddy will accuse another man at this very same bar and be shot dead where he stood for it.

We went to the bathroom and split the heroin down the middle. I shot a little for the road and hit the streets in search of my girlfriend. Her name was Malinda.

But I never found her.

Close to midnight I'd wound up at Freddy's duplex with his fiancé, a woman in whose condition had a regular sized torso, but short, gnomic arms, short, gnomic legs. I never caught the name of her condition, but she was very easy on the eyes. One thing led to another, and we were shooting more heroin. But I was in a bad sort of arrangement—having been drunk, dehydrated, not sleeping well, and not having a partner to split my half with. Right as the junk rushed into my bloodstream, my heart fluttered, and I was out cold. I thought I had been out for two, maybe three seconds. I had no idea until several days later, that it'd been over an hour that I was laying there, owing my debts to the devil. But when I peeled my eyes open, I saw Freddy and his fiancé whorling over me, doing whatever they could to work me out of limbo. My tongue was the only thing I had noticed, or felt more than anything. His fiancé was screaming, "He bit the tip of his goddamned tongue off!"

Freddy brought me up to the pneumatic doors of the Emergency entrance, carrying me inside the way a mother carries her child. "This guy, he's fucking dying here—get him some help!" Freddy begged the orderly at the station.

"I see," she said. "Okay. What seems to be the matter? What's his name?"

"I don't know," Freddy said. "I just seen this guy throwing up and having a seizure, some sort of attack out front of the Walgreens on White Sands. I think it's drugs."

And then I remember, while being lifted onto a gatch bed, seeing Freddy sprinting out the door. "Hey, get back here, buddy," an orderly called after him.

The Narcan they gave me worked, and when I finally came to for good, I saw how brilliant the room looked, like a warm cloud whose fluorescent sun cast upon me the reality of it all: that I was actually living, actually breathing. I was euphoric to not have been dead, and I realized how close I'd come to dissolving out of this world for the second time in the very same day.

Malinda on the other hand hadn't been as fortunate. As it would turn out, she'd left me forever. She'd taken up with a guy called Jack Munger. I knew this Munger guy. I'd come across this sot from a beer party out at this steer roper's house up in a place called Dog Canyon in my early twenties. Before the party got going, Munger snorted a line of coke and pressed a pistol to my temple and threatened my life because I hadn't wanted to buy any drugs off of him. When he finished his threat, he simply smiled and went away. Later at that same party, with that same gun, he silenced the entire crowd around the bonfire by firing it into the dirt so that he could listen to me play the guitar, and telling everyone with his eyes closed to listen. "Listennn," he whispered. "Listennn."

And according to legend, he'd repeated that word in the same fashion to the cops when they arrived over a concerned mother and her young daughter's welfare. Munger had opened the door, naked to his waist and slick with blood, telling the cops that she'd really done it this time.

They found her dismembered in the bathtub. My sweet, beautiful Malinda had been butchered like an animal.

It made national headlines, Munger's brutal murder, and it didn't take long for a certain brand of justice to befall him. He was sitting in the dayroom with the other inmates when coverage of the case appeared on the television. All eyes turned on him, and the guards would subsequently find his mangled corpus the following morning, in his cell, with a broom handle sticking out of his back end. His particular exit from this world wasn't what I had in mind. I'm afraid to tell you the fate I'd envisioned for him. But I suppose life isn't fair. It was never supposed to be.

A REASONABLE AMOUNT OF TROUBLE

They blast through the door of the motel room like something shot from hell. Cursing in vociferous ill-will, plate-eyed, apoplectic with rage. Cutter levels his pump-action shotgun at the man reclined on the bed. Grisly shoves past him wielding a .45 Taurus, seizes into a headlock and jams the barrel of it to the temple of the man who, until this moment, had been packing away a Walmart grocery sack with meth. A gym bag full of cash sits open beside it. "All right, goddamn," the man stammers to Grisly. His eyes watering, a thin string of drool swinging from his lower lip. Grisly says, "You little fistfuckers. This is our shit." The man who's held at gunpoint by Cutter says, "Fuck it is. Watch this."

At this juncture a man explodes from the bathroom stumbling with an H&K machine pistol and immediately opens fire at Cutter. Cutter dives to the floor. Grisly ducks, lets off three rounds, one of which scatters the brains of the man across the peeling scrollwork. The two captives bolt through the open door, the cash and shipment of meth in tow. Cutter rolls onto his back, fires between his boots a desperate load of buckshot into the wall, punching out a pan-sized window into the corridor. Smoke hangs and curls in the room.

"You hit, Cutter?"

Cutter presses his hand to his abdomen. Slick with hot blood. He is slathered in it. "Was that Goon you killed?"

"Yeah. You hit?"

"Yeah," Cutter says. "Yeah, I'm hit. Hit pretty good."

"Goddamn," Grisly says.

"They got our money."

"Sure as shit, and our product, sons of bitches."

The pair who'd gotten away were brothers, separated only by paternal blood. Carl and Jett. Two young dope-heads hired by Cutter and Grisly some months back who altogether had maybe one hemisphere of gray matter. But they were cheap labor—packs of Pall Malls, cases of Natural Light, a small sum of cash if they traversed greater distances for transactions. Earlier in the night, Cutter had gone to conduct inventory. Had a big arrangement coming up on the agenda. Somebody had made off with product. Somebody had made off with some profits. And Goon had led them straight to their motel room. What they didn't know was that Goon had orchestrated an ambush with the brothers. But now that he was dealt with, there were still two assholes on the road with their shit. Two targets who by the end of the night, would be dead. Had to be dead. But Cutter. He was in piss poor shape.

Cutter lays in a mess of gore in the passenger seat. His face is gone of blood. He clutches his gut with trembling hands, himself shuddering and coughing up blood and bile. Grisly works the wheel with one hand, the other plucks a Marlboro red from the soft pack in his breast pocket. "We'll stop by Kangas's, get you nice and fixed up," Grisly says. "You with me?" He lights his cigarette.

"I'm here." Faltering voice. A voice you might hear in another room of your house. Or where on the eve of certain calendar nights the bone rider on his bone horse pulls forth his deathcart along the streets calling the names that father death has marked for return.

"Don't you fucking worry, Cutter. We'll get you to

Kangas's and he will patch you up. Like new. Like you were put in a new body. That good." He sticks the cigarette in Cutter's lips. "Here. Smoke that. Make you feel better."

The streetlamps running past wash through the windows of the big Buick a sepulchral light. The pool of blood upon Cutter's clothes and upon the seat increasing in the intermittent voids of black. It is quiet. The night grows grim. Grisly makes a call on his cell. "Yeah. Cutter is shot. Bad. Bad enough to where he's fucking dying. Dying in my fucking car as we speak. Yeah. Be there in a few. On Oliver right now." He looks to Cutter. Cutter hasn't moved. "You all right, buddy? Buddy?"

Cutter burps from the holes the bullets have made in his torso. "What a night," he says very weakly. "What a night."

Grisly fishtails onto a residential street, shoves hard to stop in the driveway of a small house. Where the army doctor stands under the dull green glow of the garage light in wait like some doomland bodyguard. At first Grisly forgets to shift the vehicle into park, has already half gotten out, and jumps back in and jams the shifter down into park, he and Cutter lurching forward briefly.

"So he's been shot?" says Kangas ushering over to the passenger door. Grisly is hauling Cutter out by the armpits, says without looking at Kangas, "Why no, I think he's just skint his elbow."

"Damn."

"We need to get him inside."

Kangas's girlfriend barrels through the front door, the screen door slapping to. Her pink flip-flops keeping a frenzied heel slap sound. Her hands are about her cheeks. She says, "Kangas, what the hell is this? *What* the *hell* is this?"

Grisly regards Kangas crazily. "You didn't tell her we were coming?"

Kangas stares at him, mouth working open and shut, but there are no words for this derelict mind to harvest.

"You asshole."

"I thought she was asleep."

"And what about her waking up to you working on a dying man, huh?"

Kangas shrugs.

Kangas's girlfriend is now standing over this drama unfolding before her. Her arms flailing about. "Kangas! Is he dead? Who are these guys?" She shoves Grisly's shoulder. "Who are you?"

Cutter lays motionless, eyes open, the eyes about which were a glossy milkblue, they—these in attendance, windowed away in miniature therein.

"Get your fucking hand off of me," says Grisly.

Kangas swipes Grisly across the face. "Don't talk to my bitch like that."

"Oh I'm a bitch?"

Grisly—remembering a time in his youth, acquiring the regional Golden Gloves title—plants his right foot, rears back a whited fist, shifts his weight to his left leg, and snaps with his waist, a right cross which drops Kangas as if his bones had simply been vaporized from their fleshy sheathings.

It is soundless in the house. Soundless save for a television playing somewhere in the house. Screams. A chainsaw in rotary horror. Kangas is sitting on a loveseat, a bag of frozen carrots pressing against his jaw. Kangas's girlfriend is smoking weed out of the brain-cup of Batman. She chokes on the chuffs of blue smoke. Grisly is sitting slumped in an EZ chair staring placidly at Cutter's corpse who is gawking, jaw broken of hinges, at the ceiling with something of profound curiosity.

Out of this serried smoky gloom Kangas says, looking at Cutter's body, "I'm gonna have to pull this carpet. Probably the sub-flooring, too."

Grisly drags his eyes from Cutter to Kangas laboriously, says, "Kangas."

"What?"

"Nothing. Just Kangas."

Kangas's girlfriend delicately places the weed bowl

on a trash-clutched lamp table, wipes the corner of her mouth with her pinky, and says, "So how did this happen?"

No response from either party. Finally, Kangas says, "Some junkies skimmed their shit. Shit went south. That about right, Grisly?"

Grisly nods slowly.

"So then what the fuck? What the fuck do we do now? I have a dead motherfucker on my floor."

Kangas looks ponderously at Grisly. "What do we do now?"

"Well, you are gonna get rid of Cutter. I have a couple of sorry assholes to catch."

"Whoa whoa whoa," says Kangas's girlfriend, coming aright and surging forth, waving her hands, coughing deep in her chest. "That's your business, guy. Kangas here isn't getting rid of a dead body."

"Yeah—no way, man."

"Way. You let him die, you inherit the responsibility."

"Get this dead son of a bitch out of my house!"

"I've got an idea," says Grisly. He stretches his leg out, leans back into the cushion, works the .45 Taurus out of his waistband. Chambers a round, levels it at Kangas. Kangas jolts and shields both hands before his face. Index finger shaking spasmodically. Kangas's girlfriend lets out a muted shriek and sits down, covers her eyes.

"Now this is fucked," Kangas says, shying his head away.

He drove the sadder parts of Wichita, stopping in at the gambling houses. "Them? Carl and Jett? Ain't seen them, Grisly." Then going on to all the haunts and watering holes the brothers were known to frequent—Pleasures. Oasis Lounge. The Triangle Club. The Red Garter Inn. A ghoul at the Red Garter Inn said the brothers had come in earlier in the evening and were hence barred for reasons she would not name. By and by he came away empty-handed. Cutter is dead. He has killed a man his own self tonight. He is out—between product and cash—fifteen-thousand dollars cash money that he will in all likelihood never see again. He is weary, slightly drunk. He reckons this trade none too suited for him anymore.

What woke him in the small hours of morning—before any light, there was no light, save an insubstantial moon, was headlights cutting through his bedroom window. Somebody has commenced laying on a horn. He gets out of bed, grabs his pistol, peeks through the curtains. "Mother of God," he says.

Knocks at the door. He opens. Ever so slightly. "Grisly," says Kangas. His lower lip is grotesquely swollen. "We have a problem."

"Yeah we do. You're here. So leave."

"Hear me out."

Grisly rubs his face. Kangas watches him. "Well," Grisly says.

"I need a hand with Cutter."

"Leave," says Grisly, but when he attempts to shut the door, there is to be found a slipper shoe wedged between it and the jamb. "Move your foot, Kangas. I swear to fuck."

"He's in the bed of my truck."

"Lower your goddamn voice."

"Come on, Grisly. I can't do nothing with him. He's gonna stink up my truck."

"Have you tried old Wyler's yard?"

"I tried Wyler's."

"Well?"

"Well Wyler's in the penitentiary. They got new owners—help me out here, Grisly. You put me in the middle of this mess. Put me and my girlfriend right smack in the middle of a nightmare."

Grisly opens up the door fully and then drives it home into Kangas's foot.

"Ow—shit! My foot!" Kangas holds his wounded foot, does a little one-legged hop.

"Move your foot then, asshole."

"I think you broke it. I think you broke my foot."

"Kangas," Grisly says, jutting his chin toward

Kangas's truck. "What's that hitched to your truck there?"

"A woodchipper," Kangas says, bending forward, massaging the sides of his foot with his thumbs.

"A woodchipper."

"Yeah."

"It didn't cross your mind how loud those things are?"

"Hell, I'm not gonna do it here. I have a spot in mind."

"And you want me to help you put Cutter through a woodchipper. At three in the morning."

"I need the muscle, yeah. Cutter's a big boy. Come on man, you've stuck a fucked-up situation in the middle of my house."

Grisly stares at him. He thinks. After a while, he says, "All right. If I lend you a hand, we are not to speak ever again. In fact, lose my number right now. I'm signing a letter of resignation after tonight."

Grisly and Kangas on the road. They are outside the city limits now. Grisly stares out the window watching the night wheel past. "Boy," Kangas says. "It's a night dark as I've ever seen."

"Why don't you just shut up?"

Kangas cracks his neck, tightens his grip on the wheel. They drive on into further hinterlands. Doomed patrons of the witching hour.

Kangas parks in a field of tall grass. They just sit there in the cab for a handful of minutes without speaking a word. Watching like mutes the helix of insects wave on wave aspiring in the columnar lights of Kangas's old Chevy pickup.

"You know," says Grisly, not looking at Kangas. "I'm sorry about this."

"Gee, that's all right. Just surprises me how indifferent you are about all this. Well, about Cutter anyways."

"Life is indifferent to me. Why should I be otherwise with it?"

"That's some smart shit right there. I forget how you're a smart son of a bitch."

Grisly shakes his head. "Where are we?"

"I don't know. South of town. Up ahead where those trees are is the Cowskin. Used to fish there all the damn time with my brother. Got these big channel cats in there. Bigger than old Cutter back there. I was thinking about backing the woodchipper up to the edge of the creek."

"What is he in?"

"Huh?"

"What is he in? A sheet?"

"Oil drum."

Grisly stares at him inquisitively. "Do you have him strapped to the bedrail?"

Kangas scratches his stomach, says, "Naw, naw, he's just back there in an oil drum."

"I never heard an oil drum rolling around."

Kangas's jaw falls open. "Oh shit," he says and leaps out the door.

Grisly kicks open his door and wades through the grass, slapping at mosquitos, and makes his way to the rear of the truck. "Tell me he's in there, Kangas. Tell me he's in there." When he washes up at the back of the truck, he sees the tailgate down and Kangas on the other side of the truck with his arms folded over the bedrail and his face buried in his forearms. Grisly looks at him and into the bed of the truck and then out into the dark. A clamor of insects calling out in the night. Frogs somewhere. Grisly looks at Kangas. "You never put the tailgate up after you loaded him, did you."

"Dammit, no," Kangas cries.

"Well," says Grisly, he slaps his neck. "We're about twenty-five minutes out from town."

"What do you mean by that?"

"I mean if he fell out in town it's a wrap. Middle of the road. It's almost four o'clock. Roads are picking up with the factory workers."

"But if he's on the road between us and town, we didn't pass nobody."

"Exactly."

"Well."

Grisly slaps the back of his neck. "Well let's by God go look."

"You're getting all ate up by them things, man. Ain't a one got me."

"They're scared they will catch the dumbass."

Kangas hits Grisly over the chest with the back of his wrist. "There he is, old buddy."

Cutter wasn't far. Perhaps two miles north of where they had been, and he lies in the bar ditch, with just the faintest suggestion of an orange rim sticking out through the grass and blackberry briars that had taken over the ditch years past. "Good eye," Grisly says. Kangas pulls halfway off the road, cuts his lights off, and gets out. Grisly stands between the open door of the truck and the cab glancing around.

"I can't see down here," Kangas calls out.

Grisly leans into the cab and switches on the headlights. Opens up on Kangas laboring over the oil drum like a stricken ape. The shadow of Kangas and oil drum casting long and thin in the grass. "How about now?" Grisly says.

"Better," says Kangas. "Better."

"That's the one?"

"This is the one. Can you come down here and give me a hand, buddy?"

Grisly descends into the bar ditch and what he sees when he gets to the oil drum almost leaves him breathless. "What?" Asks Kangas.

"Was the oil drum all beat up when you had it or found out or wherever you'd gotten it from?"

"Why?"

"Because it's beat up and there's paint scratched on it."

Kangas observes the drum. "Hell, it does look like somebody hit it, doesn't it?"

There is blood leaking from the bottom seal.

"Shit," says Grisly.

"Don't fret man, if somebody was concerned, they'd have stayed, I'm sure. Stayed and waited for the cops, I'm sure. Here, help me out—you get that side."

They are mid-ascent when the police car whines to a halt behind the woodchipper. "If that isn't the drizzlin shits," says Kangas.

"Just shut up. I mean it, shut up."

Door opens, Maglite opens up the night, polished shoes crunching in the gravel headed their way. They stand like cats, watching the officer advance. Then the beam falls upon them. Two pathetic miscreants caught in the act of further dumbassery. "Morning, boys," the cop says.

Kangas assumes a good-natured smile. "Officer," he says.

"What have you got there?"

"Oh justa—"

"A dead body," Grisly breaks in.

Kangas gives Grisly a venomous look. "What the hell?" He spits under his breath.

The officer chuckles. Stands above them playing the light upon the oil drum and upon their upturned faces and then at the road edge. A thumb was hooked in his belt. "Well," the officer begins. "There was a young gal called about a mysterious object in the middle of the road. Coming back from a birthday party, said she was, and she ran into something went skittering off into this here bar ditch. I take it, it belongs to you?"

Kangas shakes his head no.

Grisly studies the cop, says nothing. He knows what's next.

"Mind if I have me a look inside?"

Sentencing wasn't until winter of the year next. He was convicted on the murder of David Ray Allen, also known on the street as Goon. And he was convicted on charges of concealment of a corpse and tampering with evidence. And lastly, he was convicted on the conspiracy to traffic narcotics.

Taking a plea would reduce his sentence one hundred years. Leaving him with life without the possibility of parole. A decorated felon, he. He stood no chance. He spent three months in the Sedgwick County jail before being transferred to the state penitentiary. He took classes on law, he started a book club. He seemed none too phased by his new life. Perhaps he'd known this was his fate. Perhaps since the night of his conception, he was fated by a celestial hand.

One month before his sentencing there was a prisoner newly extradited. Grisly hardly recognized him at first. Grisly, on this evening, was playing dominos with a few inmates at one of the steel tables in the recreation area of the pod. He watched this newcomer through his brows. "Come here," Grisly had said. The newcomer came. The newcomer sat. "Have you ever played dead man walking, Carl?"

OUROBOROS

I was hiding out with Joe Dooley at his godforsaken apartment because a man, a big, big man, this Blanchard man whom I feared immensely, had a bounty out for my head. I was eighteen, nineteen, somewhere around there. I'd just dropped out of community college and fled my folks' home. So here I was, seeking asylum at Dooley's grand, roach infested palace, ingesting or injecting whatever drugs we could get our vile, degenerate hands on, while my father drove around town seeking my whereabouts. In the meantime, though, this night, we drove around looking for enough stuff to put us under forever. I'd decided for no reason at all that this life wasn't worth it. You couldn't take things, your legacy, with you into the earth anyways—that was my thinking then. As for Dooley, it was his marital problems. He was a decade or better older than me, and I wanted to be just like him.

But we were broke. That was problem number one.

"That fucking child support," Dooley said. He was sitting on the sofa smoking the duck end of a cigarette. His fingertips were all the time yellowed with nicotine. "Would you believe it? She fucks around on me and expects me to pay for some other prick's nutling."

"I don't know man," I said. We had done some blotter acid earlier at this lovely lady's New Year's Eve party and the effects were beginning to set in—the drop ceiling tiles were making some interesting displays, some Rorschach patterns. The music on the radio, I remember actually riding Clapton's guitar licks like a surfer catching a big wave. Anyway, we were wondering how we could come up with some money, some free drugs. Like I said, we didn't just want to get high. We wanted to fucking die on top. "What about Bono?" I said, watching my hand split into three as I waved it about slowly.

"What about Bono? What the fuck about him? Who the fuck is Bono? The U2 guy?"

"You know," I said. I actually could not recall Bono's real name. We'd just known the guy as Bono. Some guys in the gutter system we lived in—that many of our kind lived in, had these nicknames, these effectual names that perhaps kept them only from recognition from cops.

Something like that. Anyway, Bono. That was the guy. He'd always been good to us. On a pinch he'd been known to lend us some of his mother's luminal barbiturates, and for us, at least for that night, would be a start. "The short guy, lives by Tulie Creek," I continued. "You know who I'm talking about. Don't look at me like that, you know who I'm talking about."

Dooley looked at me with skillet sized eyeballs. "Man," he said. "Hey. What are those little monkeys called?"

"That's right," I said, suddenly being assailed with an epiphany. "Yeah man, yeah. He's got a monkey; I had forgotten all about that. The weird fucker has a monkey, man. Capuchin. A goddamned Capuchin monkey. That's what he's got. I know who you're talking about now. Bono. Bono the monkey man. Has that little creature on his shoulder everywhere he goes."

So we were on the road. The diode numerals on the radio read 8:35. The fireworks were going in the sky; nebulas detonating in magnificent ribbons of fiery spectra— whole galaxies coming to their cataclysmic end. We made our way through the edge of our town, down along by these dilapidated shacks, these warrens of the damned. Bono's world. Our world.

I held my arm out the window, slicing through the bitter wind with the blade of my hand.

"Roll that damn window up," Dooley hissed. "It's hellaciously cold."

"But man, listen. You see this?"

"Oh. I've gotten the button here."

"Dooley rolled the window up."

It felt like we'd been driving for an eternity, but I was suddenly sobered up by a familiar, an all too familiar person, idling in their grumbling Camaro next to us at the light. I slid down in the seat, white knuckling the undercarriage of it. I'd never been so frightened in my life. Shit.

"Fuck," I said.

"What's your problem? You're supposed to be in a good mood on this stuff. A happy mood."

"That guy right there, beside us, is Blanchard."

"Who the fuck is Blanchard?"

"The guy who wants to take my head off. Cut down this way."

Then Dooley, being the maniac that he had the proclivity to be, reached under his seat and produced a huge gun.

"Go man, go," I screamed. "Put that thing down."

"I'm gonna ventilate this asshole," Dooley said, snapping the slide back, pushing the little button to descend the window down the channel. But by the grace of whatever, fate—although I'm not too fond of that word—the light flicked on green, and Blanchard went on his merry way, rattling the whole car as he went.

"What's your deal with Blanchard? He catch you screwing his girl?"

"I owe him a lot of money. A lot."

"How much is a lot?"

"Two-hundred bucks."

"Oh shit."

We wound our way down this dirt road flanked by

monstrous mesquite and creosote bushes; we were pretty well into the country by now, and by now the blotter had taken full effect.

"Right here," I said to Dooley. "The one with the blue porch light. The really fucking bright one. Jesus Christ why's it so bright."

Dooley pumped the brakes, and we swung up the weed grown drive. The house itself reared out of the darkness like a huge slug. Dooley put the car in park. "Go up and knock on the door," Dooley said.

"You're not coming with me?"

"I am. Yeah. Give me a minute."

So I got out. I walked up to the door and knocked three times. Almost immediately, it opened up very slightly and, in the gap, I saw the face of a beautiful woman. Perhaps the most beautiful woman ever.

"Hello?"

"Yeah, Is Bono around?"

"Who's Bono?"

"Is this not his house? This should be his house. He's got a monkey. You know, little capuchin monkey."

"I don't know who Bono is."

"Well, did he move or something?"

"I've already told you. I don't know who you're talking about. Do you need help? Are you okay?"

"You are totally gorgeous. Drop dead gorgeous."

But the door banged shut. Back in the car, I could see that Dooley had developed a condition. A very bad one. He'd apparently vomited all over his lap and was holding his hands palm up as someone would do when hauling a load of firewood. "Sicky," he cried. "Sicky sick sick."

"We need to get you to a hospital," I said.

"No. Fuck that. They'll arrest me."

"How much did you take?"

"I think I'm dying, man."

I don't remember what I said next, but I ran back to the house and beat the door. "Call an ambulance," I yelled. "This man is dying." Then the door opened up, and I was peering into the big black bore of what looked like a cannon.

"You need to leave."

"But my friend."

"Yessir. This man is trying to break into my house." There was another lady, I couldn't see her, behind the lady I'd just spoken to, on the phone with the cops.

"You all are a bunch of bitches," I hissed before making it to the car again. I pulled Dooley out of the driver seat, and just as I'd gotten hold of his collar, he sprayed a jet of puke all over my chest. "I'm dying man, I'm dying here."

"Come on," I said, dragging him by the armpits to the passenger side. "You're not going to die." I managed the door open and stuffed him into the cab and ran and got under the wheel and cranked the engine and flicked on the headlights. As I cranked the wheel, the cones of lights swept across the two women like storefront mannequins standing shouldered on the porch and then we were gone.

He was falling unconscious now. I punched his shoulder, and he jerked alive. "Hello, God? Am I dead?"

"You're not dead. You're just really high. What else did you take?"

He did not answer. In fact, he fell out of consciousness again and slapped his skull against the window. All the while my ass and chest were soaked in his abdominal discharges. It was still very warm, and it took everything within my power not to contribute. I just wanted to get this over with, just get home and shower forever. Never mind Bono, never mind Blanchard. I was swearing off this life for good. But it didn't happen for a very long time.

We were on the highway now, barreling down the night. The nearest hospital was in the next town, some fifteen minutes away. We were just coming into the town's limits when Dooley was resurrected, sat up straight, and said, with total clarity, "Are you hungry? I'm hungry. We should get a burger."

"What? We're going to the hospital, man. You're puking everywhere."

"I feel fine. I feel great. Wonderful, in fact."

Maybe he was right. Maybe all he'd needed was something to eat after all. I pulled into one of the stalls at

Sonic and ordered burgers and fries.

"I get like this on acid," he said. Staring numbly out of his face at the little building.

"Well maybe you should quit. You've thrown up all over your car and on me."

"Sorry about that."

Then the sound. That grumbling. Blanchard's Camaro pulled in two slots away from us.

I eyeballed whatever I could see of his car and felt under the seat for Dooley's pistol.

"When's the food going to get here?" Dooley asked, still not looking anywhere but the building.

"Soon," I said. I fished the gun out. I'd never actually held a gun before, I didn't even know how to use one. It was heavier than I'd imagined. The movies make them seem light. But I was a scrawny and again eighteen or nineteen then with something to prove. Anyway, I'd thought that maybe with it buried in his face, the gun, that it might have been enough to scare dog shit out of him. I could hear him now, God that stupid little voice.

"Hang tight," I told Dooley. Unbothered, he nodded like some lobotomy recipient. Then I gripped the gun hard and put my hand on the door handle and opened the door. "Two garlic butter bacon cheeseburger meals with two large Cokes?" the carhop lady said. Where had she come from? I certainly hadn't heard the wheels of her skates. She simply just appeared like an apparition. I looked up at her and closed the door and stuck the gun very carefully between the seats. "Yes ma'am," I said.

She handed over the two bags of food and the drinks through the window.

"Look at you, goodness almighty, what's all over you?"

Embarrassed, I peeled a five out of my wallet and proffered it to her. She held the bill aloft like it were a dirty sock. "Why's it all wet?"

I said nothing, just rolled the window up and stared at her until she skated away. Back to Blanchard. He was still sitting there, the Camaro chugging along.

"Sorry I threw up all over you, man," Dooley said, cheeks full of burger.

"It's all right," I said. I wasn't even hungry. After all I had this man's vomit soaking into my flesh. I turned over and emptied the bag of food onto the center console. Fries fell everywhere.

"Hey, what the hell," Dooley said. "What are you doing?"

I punched two eye holes into the bag with my thumb. "Blanchard. He's right over there."

"I'm going to teach him not to fuck with me."

"You're what? What are you going to do?"

Then I draped the bag over my head—it splitting down the sides and back like an upturned banana peel, but somehow holding enough integrity to stick to my little skull—and got the gun and climbed out of the car. Walking, I could feel my heart shunting blood inside my ears, it was magnificent. Joe's vomit had crystallized on my shirt in winter's spiteful grip and oddly, very oddly, I was burning up.

I came up from the rear of his car and slid between the ordering panel and his window. The hulking figure was smoking a cigarette. He looked first at the gun and then up at me. He smiled. "What the fuck are you?" Blanchard said with a smooth, deferential voice. Then I stuck the gun, trembling, not because I was terrified, not because I was cold, but because the gun was simply very heavy, through the window and leveled it at his fat, repugnant face. I said, "You don't know me, but you're after a guy I know, a guy who happens to be a very good associate of mine, and you've so happened to fuck with the wrong set of people."

He let out this god-awful laugh and gripped my wrist, jerked me toward him. I hit my head against the door so hard that my entire field of vision had been bleached a perfect white for a few seconds. I hadn't seen him do it, but I felt his own gun dig into my cheek, crackling the paper bag over my head. "I ought to blow your goddamned brains all over this goddamned place."

What could I have said at this juncture?

"I don't know who the fuck you think you are

putting a gun in my face, but you're badly mistaken, bud. Here I am, treating my little son to an ice cream and you want to go about putting a gun in my face."

Then, out of nowhere, I heard this earth-rending *whap*. We, Blanchard and I, spun our heads. It was Dooley. He'd brought a baseball bat from the trunk of the car and had set about beating the hell out of Blanchard's car with it. Blanchard's son in the backseat was screaming now. "Motherfucker!" Dooley yelled, swinging like a batter going for the outfield. He busted out the back passenger window, showering the poor child in a million bits of glass. Just then, with my attention drawn on Dooley, Blanchard pinned me between the ordering panel with his door, sucking the breath right up out of me and succeeded this by fetching a hellacious crack up top of my head with the hilt of his gun. Blood ran hotly all down my face, completely soaking the sack over my head. The boy screaming, Blanchard going full tilt after Dooley. Everybody's breath exploding in the cold like battlesmoke. But I was the one with the gun. I'd never understood that; why he was more concerned about Dooley and his ball bat rather than me with a gun. Perhaps he knew I wouldn't really do anything with it. And looking back, perhaps he was dead right. I couldn't see by this point for the blood, God how the head does bleed, but I felt somebody's hand grip my shoulder and tear me free like a dog saved from drowning in a river. Just do it, I was thinking, just put that gun to my head and squeeze that trigger with everything you've got and don't let up until that magazine is empty.

"We need to skedaddle," I heard Dooley's faltering voice say. "I think I killed him."

I peeled the blood-sogged sack off my head. The boy was still squalling, and somebody was hushing him. A few yards away, attended by some people, I could see Blanchard's gigantic corpus laying on the pavement convulsing.

"What?" I said. "What?"

"I got him over the head, man. I hit him in the goddamn head with a baseball bat."

Dooley proceeded just then to unpin me, and we

hightailed it to his car. Some years later as it would turn out, Blanchard had in fact not perished at the hands of Joe Dooley, but rather went on to become a respected and very knowledgeable drugs and alcohol counselor, albeit with a slight limp.

We'd just swung out of the lot and were back on the highway when the lights flared on behind us. "I can't go back to jail," Dooley cried. "I've got a whole future ahead of me." Then he mashed the accelerator to the floorplate. What do you do in that situation? What can you do other than grip the grab handle and pray for the best? That's what I did. Dooley was goosing it down the highway, the little nimbuses of streetlamps all blurred together without definition. It was quite magical actually. Once you learn to accept your fate, life becomes rather tolerable. At least it did until Dooley stamped the brakes, and we screeched to a halt on the shoulder of some little road. "What are you doing?" I cried. "We're already committed. We're outlaws."

Defeated, Dooley placed his hands gently upon the wheel. "I can't live like this," he said to it, the wheel. "And besides, the tank is at less than an eighth."

Our faces washed red to blue in the cab, like the systole and diastole of fate. I could see in the wing mirror an armed patrolman coming up to Dooley's side of the car. He was crying inconsolably now, Dooley was. He rolled down the window laboriously.

"Step out of the car," the officer said, his service weapon viciously looking us down with its awful black eye. "You too. Both of you." Dooley lifted his hands from the wheel and graciously opened his door and got out. As for me, I just sat there, paralyzed with fear's formidable grip. I watched the road ahead of me. The dual yellow eyes of headlamps chugging in the opposite lane. This is it. I've already a bench warrant out for my arrest—contempt of court for failing to appear for Jury Duty.

Then there was a commotion, a scuffle, and the police cruiser went whizzing by like a particolored smear, leaving me in total darkness. I looked back and glimpsed the officer climbing to his feet in the road. "Oh shit, Dooley," I said aloud, and perhaps just loud enough to remind the officer that I was still inside the cab. He began to trot over to the car. But I leaned and pressed my fist on the brake and with the other hand, shifted into drive and punched the accelerator and off I went. I maneuvered over into the driver seat and gunned it through the streets feeling much invigorated and wishing I could do this all over again for the rest of my life—that's how magnificent this particular experience had been for me.

I laid low for a little while before ditching Dooley's car in someone's driveway. I quit the neighborhood and crossed this barren desert lot and, wondrously enough, came out into the parking lot of Roller City—the popular roller skate establishment of this town, one in which I'd spent many a night as a small child. I stood studying the edifice with my teeth chattering, reminiscing on old, fond times of my youth, only to discover, when I'd turned to go, my father and my little brother exiting the building with plastic smiles. But those smiles vacated, and their mouths assumed an astonished gape when they saw me approach them, bloodied and with frozen vomit all down my shirt. "Hey dad," I said.

WATER THROUGH A SIEVE

From where I'm sitting you can see the stunted skyline of this midwestern city. The window looks out directly over the street. A few families are walking along the sidewalks, smiling, their faces shining like plastic dolls. It's sunny, blue sky, and from what I can tell, no wind. A few small birds swoop down, hop around on the whitewashed window ledge. They aren't there long, and they take flight, and *poof*, they're gone. Far off, standing blue and enigmatic in the distance, I see the looming steel statue of the Keeper praying over the fork in the river. I try to imagine the ancients lighting council fires there on the knoll. I wonder what their world must have looked like. It couldn't have looked like this one.

    I glance around and it's as if everything in this room had been on pause while my gaze was fixed through the window, and now everything has seemingly resumed production again; I see medical people shifting around, people laughing, talking, crying, TVs going, and then I look back out through the window. I breathe deep, scan for more birds somewhere in that vast expanse of blue. I like moments like those, moments of getting lost looking through the window, watching the clouds, the birds, chart the sky. It helps to forget, or anyway, distract from the fact that I'm dying.

I notice this guy, this older guy—not much older than me, but a little—he sits down in the pleather recliner next to me. There's something strikingly familiar about him. After covertly glancing through the corner of my eye while an attractive nurse attaches IV cocktails to him, I notice his features are a lot like the features of a friend of mine that I haven't seen in here since I started chemo a week ago—Olin. It's Swedish. This guy has got curly graying gold hair, a white stubble, nordic blue eyes—he's even wearing the same circular wire rim glasses, or rather they appear to be the same anyway, as Olin's. I know it's not him. I really know it's not, but I can't help but to wonder about him.

I think I'll give him a call. I have his number saved in my phone.

All right. I call his number. After two rings, a woman picks up. Olin's wife. She cries to me, "Hello? Filip?"

"This isn't Filip,"—and I inform her that it's me. I can tell right off by the tone of her voice that something had happened. Something awful. My heart is punching my eardrums. "I have to let you go; I'm very sorry. It's just … Olin," and she moans horrifically. "What about him? What about Olin?" "He… Olin went—" and another detonation of weeping. "Please, I beg, please tell me what happened to him." "He just went into the shower, just now, and shot himself," she sobs. "He's dead! He's dead!" I have a hard time absorbing that. I ask her to say again what she'd just told me, hoping, desperately, that perhaps I'd misheard her, but to my horror, it was exactly what I'd feared I'd heard. I have nothing to say. I can't get my brain to let anything out of my mouth. "I'm sorry," she says. "But I have to let you go now—I have a father to call—a sister—I'm sorry … I'm sorry," and the line was cut.

I shove my phone into my pocket, look out the window again. I can only imagine what it's like to make that sort of phone call to family. Cancer is already a hard enough call to make, I get that, but an unexpected passing, to that magnitude…

The sun burns like a magnesium flare, throws its heat up at me from the asphalt. When I get to my car, and crank the engine, I can almost feel my lashes and brows melt off by the blast of hot air coming from the AC. I keep forgetting that. I remind myself to get it checked out, knowing I'll forget. I roll down the window glass, back out of the parking slot and start the drive back home.

Driving along the oxbow of the Arkansas river, I think about my ex-wife, whom of which I'd been living with, until today, and of whom, after some months back, quit her job waiting tables at Denny's, and stopped making payments on the house—once she found out none of us could afford to stay in it if the other one jets. We both move around the house trying to keep out of the other's way. The house is rigged up with tripwires and land mines. One misstep and *blam* we're at each other's throats like feral cats. It's as if we're holding our breaths, as if there's not enough oxygen to be shared.

Her name is Laura.

We were married for five insane years and put a stop to it half a year ago following a string of affairs. Of which she'd admitted had gone on practically the length of our entire marriage. But it all converged that day I found them in the back of his car, in front of our house, with the sun seeping through the windows of his brand-new Buick. I guess for her there was no thrill anymore. They had to get caught.

On 54, I run into heavy traffic. It's backed up well over half a mile, so I slow the car down to a crawl, then watch as the speedometer needle lands at zero. I see emergency lights winking far off, disjointed in the heat and swimming in shimmering red to blue heat-ghosts. I drift into the reoccurring daydream I've been having lately, the goodbye theatric wherein I press the accelerator to the floor plate and slam into an abutment, exploding into an incredible display of flames and eternal relief. I wonder if Olin had similar daydreams, and maybe that is why he did what he did this afternoon. Dealt with the cancer on his own terms.

Not that I ever would—but it gives me the creeps that I can't shake these thoughts. My Oncologist, doctor Colborne, says it's quite a common occurrence for people in my situation to fantasize about. The other day I'd admitted to him that I'm utterly terrified about what's coming. I told him that I'd never dreamt of the moment I'd really have to prepare for something such as this, such as actually dying, and I'd thought that I'd be doing things much more differently than I am right now. But I suppose you never know what you'd do until the Grim Reaper himself finally reaches your door.

The traffic begins to decongest and all of the vehicles inch ahead slowly like the pedipalps of some great arthropod. And of course, all of us—well speaking for myself I suppose—turn our heads to look at the carnage that lay next to us. There's only one reason anyone looks: to see something horrifically bad.

It's a wreck. Way up on the shoulder, I see a sportster bike all accordioned like a crumpled pop can, the rest of which lay scattered in millions of blue and black bits all around the boiling blacktop. The line of vehicles roll forward a few feet, and now through the passenger window, I see the car that had struck the motorcycle. The occupant behind the wheel had evidently slammed into the biker at such speed that the hood of which is sucked inward at a V shape. Like he headonned a telephone pole or something, that's how bad this collision had been. I can see where the life had been stolen. I won't tell you much more than that. Some uniformed deputies are directing traffic with pale, numb faces while these paramedics, veiled partially behind the guardrail, work on the victim. Then, rather quickly, they stop, arise real sullenly, and get out the gurney from the box of the ambulance, and unfold it. They move quite unlike that from what you would see in the movies. There is nothing angelic, or swift in their steps. And it occurs to me that there is nothing to be swift about. There is nothing to be saved.

The man who struck the victim is kneeling, and weeping, and I guess praying, at the guardrail. Meanwhile those of us in transit watch this catastrophe unfold like it's the climax of our dull, insignificant lives. And for some, it probably is.

But what are the words of his prayer? I think I'd like to ask him that, that man at the guardrail, but I know it would frighten me if I heard what came out of his mouth.

I pull into the driveway of our little clapboard house. I'm surprised to see that Laura is still here. She's watching out through the parted curtains of the big bay picture window, waiting, but I know it's not for me. I kill the motor and get out.

I step into the foyer. Laura doesn't say anything. She's just sitting in a wicker chair drinking—during this hour—what's probably her fifth or sixth Red Bull Vodka by now. She once filled in her clothes, looked real good on her, the weight. Now her bones are brailed under the clothes that contain her. But I suppose I've lost a good bit of mine as well. I say, "Hey."

She's quiet a moment. Then says, "Hey yourself."

"I didn't expect you'd still be here."

"Momma's driving in from Dodge City."

"I can take you."

"She's already on her way. What sense is there in telling her to turn around and you taking me? Hey mother, my ex-husband, yes, that one, is going to take me to your house, says to tell you hi!"

I want to remind her that she was the one having the affair. I can only imagine what her mother thinks of me.

"You don't have to act like that about it," I say. She's just old, she doesn't need to drive all this way."

"She's perfectly fine. She can come get me if she pleases. It's not your job to see that I'm taken care of."

"Was for a handful of years."

Now, for the first time, she shifts her eyes up at me. They are red with inebriation, like two carnelian marbles.

"Was ain't now," she says, enunciating every word clearly and cruelly.

I don't reply, just walk off into the kitchen, fix a whiskey on the rocks, then step out onto the back deck. A warm breeze riffles through the leaves, and the latticed creeper fronds quiver on the fence. I sit on one of the patio chairs, sip on the whiskey, and feel the ice cubes bump coldly against my lip. I slip my phone out of my pocket, make a call. Laura's mother answers. "Hello?"

The cicadas begin their evening songs in the trees, and it reminds me of soft summer nights with Laura by the river. In the early days when I'd believed, in my heart, that she was sent from Andromeda. Then to piss on the whole thing is none other than a faceless man. Why did I have to find out the way that I did? In *his* car in *our* driveway? Christ. I picture stuffing both of them inside a blistering furnace. The screams. Their flesh caught fire and seared through.

I walk back inside, sling the ice from my empty glass into the sink, get the bottle of Wild Turkey down from atop the refrigerator. I tilt the bottle back, work the whiskey down my throat. The day is dying in a blazing, spectacular kind of way. The treetops and roofs of neighboring houses look like ink running up to the sun. I take another pull and get out a package of pork chops from the refrigerator. I hear Laura walk through the threshold and into the kitchen. I get out a skillet, put it on the stove grate. She nudges past me to the counter, pours more vodka into her cup. These days have reduced us—not just her—into gibbering alcoholics. I'll admit that. I've lost all my shame. I click on the burner, add a chunk of butter to melt. I tear open the package and carefully place the thin meat into the skillet. "You can be honest with me, a little bit, for once," I say to the back of her skull. I flip the pork chops with a pair of tongs. She whips around. "About what?"

"About your mother coming to get you. About a number of things besides."

"What makes you think she isn't"

"A lot of things," I say, and take a swig from the Turkey. "Mostly because she told me she wasn't. She told me she didn't know what I was talking about. I had to inform her we even got a divorce."

"You called my mom? You called my mom, and told her things that are none of her business?"

"I'd say her daughter being divorced is her business, yeah, I'd say that."

"You're a sorry piece of shit, you know that?" she says, drunkenly, trying to get a rise out of me.

"I just want you to be honest with me."

"If we're divorced, I don't see that it matters. In fact, I think you'd better mind your *fucking* business."

"Like when I caught you screwing that guy in front of our house?"

"Oh you're so high and goddamn mighty."

"I'm just trying to cook us dinner, Laura."

"I didn't ask you to cook anything for me."

"Yeah yeah yeah yeah," I say, shaking grains of salt onto the meat. "You'd just rather drink yours up."

"I guess you aren't familiar with the word hypocrite, are you?"

"Guess not, no."

"Just don't make me anything, if you don't want to."

"It's almost done," I say, adding two cloves of garlic.

"But you don't want to."

I bring two plates out from the drying rack, set them side by side. "I got your plate right here."

"You can't make me eat it."

"I fixed this up for you!" I yell, then close my eyes, shake my head. I fell for her game like a fish on bait.

"If that's the way you feel about it, then I certainly don't want anything."

"I cooked this because I want you to eat." I tong a pork chop onto her plate, hear her sigh and groan. "Look, I don't even say anything and you get that angry, look at you," she mocks.

I say nothing.

"Aw, now he's pissed, now he won't talk to me."

At the dinner table, I slice a cube of meat, fork it into my mouth. Laura is clutching her cup of Red Bull Vodka like a religious relic. I say, "Please, can you eat?" She hasn't touched a thing on her plate.

"I won't eat with someone who talks to me like you do, like you continue to do, like you've always done."

Chewing, I say, "Fine, okay, don't eat then. Starve. I really could care less. But I tell you what, I wanted to cook you a good meal, and if you won't eat it, then I'll save it for me to eat tomorrow," and I get up from my seat, walk around the table to grab her plate, but when I get hold of it, she squeezes my wrist. "What are you doing! I was going to eat that!"

I see that tears are tracking down her cheeks. I give in, let go of the plate and slump back down in my chair. I feel a wave of nausea well in my stomach, passes. She saws a big block of meat with the knife, stuffs her face with it.

"Is it good?" I say.

"Is what good?" she says, working her jaw with great somnambulant movements.

"Forget it, never mind."

"Jesus H. Christ. Don't ask a question and not make clear what you're asking."

"The food. Dinner."

"Why didn't you just ask that?"

"I did. I figured you'd get what I was asking. Looks like you're enjoying it, is all."

"Am I not supposed to be enjoying it or something?"

"Here we go, I say."

"My God, you are just absolutely determined not to let me eat."

"I'm done," I say, slamming the silverware down onto the table. I get up, grip the bottle of Wild Turkey.

"Where are you going?" she says, her tone now very sweet, very compassionate.

"To bed. And I'm staying there until your little

boyfriend picks you up."

"You rotten prick! Asshole!"

I say nothing, just walk away, and trudge up the steps to the master bedroom. Because of the whiskey, room is rocking a little. I shed my boots, climb sort of unsteadily onto the bed. I find the remote, turn on the TV. Leno makes the crowd laugh. I know there is a sign that lights up, cueing the crowd to laugh. There has to be. My head is swimming. For a reason I cannot tell you, I have a memory of being a child, and I remember the first time I'd really regretted something. But I don't remember what it is I did. I only remember the crushing feeling of regret. And the fear of a life not yet lived. I think too much.

A little later, I see Laura's silhouette emerge in the doorframe. She totters to the bed, crawls in. The light of the television flickers across us. She runs her fingers through my hair, makes me tremble. I hear her sniffle away tears. "I'm sorry," she whispers. But I feel way too mean to say anything. It's silent a long time.

"Is it a new guy or the same one?" I ask finally.

She is a long time in answering. "Same one," she admits.

"Do you love him?"

"Yes," she says, running a hand down my thigh.

"When's he going to get here?"

"Soon," and she pulls herself closer. She grabs the remote, clicks off the TV. She doesn't wait. She slides her capri's off, her thong. She unbuckles my belt and yanks my Levi's down to my ankles. She straddles me. She isn't making love, this is a fuck. All right, have a fuck. I close my eyes, think of the nurse from this morning. Laura isn't here in this room, not anymore, it's the nurse that was tending to Olin's doppelgänger. Then, suddenly amid this rut, I wind up above her, becoming the arbiter of this event. I've never felt this way in my entire life. I feel like God. She whimpers, like a tiny creature. My body quakes and shudders, then after, she curls in a ball at the edge of the bed. I reach out a hand and touch her. She feels like nothing at all.

I say, "You don't have to go," I want to be stronger,

but I can't.

"Don't," she says. "Please don't," and she pushes herself off the bed, dresses. I arch my back to hike up my pants. I stare a long time at the shadows behind her eyes. She is someone I married a long time ago, and for a moment her name is lost to me.

I hear a horn blow from the driveway. We don't know what to say to each other. She extends the handle of her suitcase, wheels it to the door. She stops just short of the doorway. She is waiting for me to say something, perhaps call her back, plead for her to stay. But the room is the same: dark and loudly quiet. I stare at the black oval of her head long enough for it to boil and undulate in the darkness. I hear her shutting away her tears again, but I don't feel any way about it.

The horn blows again.

"You'd better get on," I say. "He's waiting on you." She hangs her head, says nothing, and walks out through the door, wheeling behind her the suitcase we took on our honeymoon all those years ago.

I hear the front door close, and beyond that, the storm door clap to on its keeper spring. I hear the roar of exhaust as it echoes off the sleeping streets, dissipates, and soon I hear nothing save the measured pumps of my heart inside my head. I am very tired, think how I'll never live through a day like this ever again probably. I take a swig from the bottle and set it back on the bedside table, and try to sleep.

But I can't sleep. I toss and writhe under the sheets. The hell with it. I think I'll go for a walk. I climb out of bed, throw on a dirty white tee shirt, stay in the Levi's, slip my feet into discount store moccasin slippers, and set out for a hike. I leave the porch light burning, see all the other lights of houses burning in the night. I think how there are some pretty nice homes in my neighborhood, of colonial construction. But soon, I don't know how soon, the bank will take over the house. And I will never again see this neighborhood. I'll go back home for just this night, but I have eyes to wander all across this country. I might even venture down into Mexico. I'm not sure yet. I walk on, feel the loose gravel on the street gutter crunch under my slipper soles. I am not afraid. I've got a whole other life to live.

I keep thinking about Olin and the wreck on the highway. About how the world just keeps revolving whether you're a part of it or not. It's just the way it is.

Are you like me? Do you catalogue and store away moments in your life—moments of great pleasure, or moments of dread, anguish, fear, moments of absurdity, and so on?

Then you walk in that hour of the night in which no clock names, in your sleepware, and walk far off from your usual street, down along a trough of closed storefronts, watch as you ripple from one darkened pane to another, and you stop, look in on your ghost in the glass, and you see your face turning back every moment of your life like the reel of a slot machine, and then you climb atop the railing on the bridge spanning the river and before you leap you think: *I was alive.*

THE CHAINTHROWER

The sun fired the saddle of low hills where it sat like blown glass and the drilling mud from the Kelly rig made them look like clay effigies. Rowland blinked, ran a gloved hand across his face. There were no two clean parts of him with which to clear the mud from his eyes. Three months ago a young boy out of Oklahoma had been killed, and they were still yet discovering pieces of him (or merely speculating such) in odd places about the rig floor. Rowland, while working with a drilling outfit in West Texas, had been called in by his uncle for replacement. This was better pay, he'd decided, and closer to home anyway, to the wife who was soon to quit him.

Rowland released the hook, sent it swinging up the elevator. He turned to Gummy who was catching a quick drink of water. "So tell me what happened with that roughneck."

Gummy moved into position. "We was swabbin a well near Hobbs, and I heard this awful sound on the derrick, knew that wasn't no good." The derrickman clamped the hook to the next thirty-foot section of pipe. Gummy squinted an eye heavenward, watching the derrickman. "So I booked it over the side rail," he said. "And when I was some good distance away, I looked back and seen this poor kid all mangled up in the wench drum."

The traveling block lowered the section of pipe. "Jesus Christ," Rowland said, kicking in the slips to grip the pipe.

"Yessir." Gummy unlatched the hook, sent it up again while Rowland clamped the tong to the pipe and then dallied a length of chain around the joint. In one hand, he hauled back on the chain, and in his off hand, spooned dope onto the threads as Gummy guided the next section of pipe to fit into the joint. They made the connection and Rowland slapped chain against the new section of pipe and the cathead from the drawworks rapidly spun the chain around the pipe, drawing it fiercely taut, torquing the threads tight into the joint. He carefully fed the slack, for he did not want to lose another finger.

"Eat," Came from the doorway of the doghouse. As Rowland removed his crash-hat to wipe sweat and decades old drilling mud from his face, he saw his uncle Les return through the door and into the doghouse.

"You bring anything?" Gummy wanted to know.

"Awe, just a sandwich."

"My old lady packed me some tamales, and some damn good pinto beans."

"Pinto beans in this heat? You're a brave man."

They sat about the rig and lunched. Rowland wasn't hungry but forced a few bites down fitfully.

"What are we drilling through here, shale? Jesus." Rowland could hear the derrickman, Glenn, above in the deck. "We ain't hardly making no progress through this shit. Drill tip's dulling out. People dying. Hell."

"We ain't supposed to discuss the particulars of workplace fatalities on the job," the operator said.

"I ain't on the clock. Lunch time is my time. Plain and simple."

From the door of the doghouse at the end of the catwalk swept up a belly laugh among a small group making their way to the rig floor. It made Rowland's muscles seize.

"I'm fixin to knock that Porter's head in with a rock one of these days," said Rowland, looking out toward the advancing group, chewing woodenly.

Gummy spooned beans into his mouth. "Was it what he'd told about Mia?"

Rowland flung the rest of his sandwich spinning out into the desert. He spat between his boots. "Somethin like that," he said.

Pulling on his gloves and lifting his crash-hat to his head, he heard the small group laugh again, and now on the rig floor with the rest of the crew, he heard Porter's voice say, "Ask Billy, he'll tell you all about it."

Rowland felt fire in his limbs. "I'll tell you what?"

"Is your Mia gal sure enough turning tricks behind the Flying J?"

"Fuck you, Porter."

"Whoa now, Sam's the one asked." Porter had a look on his face with something of mischievous malevolence. "She tell you how big I am, though?"

Rowland pulled off his crash-hat. But before he could fetch a fist Porter-ward, Gummy launched up from where he was sitting and jerked Rowland back by the elbow. "Don't be stupid, man," he said.

"Come on down to Cal's Shade tonight," Porter said. "I'll stomp your ass."

"Come on, boy's," Les hollered, waddling up the catwalk. "Let's act like grown men here." He whistled at the operator. "Fire her up, let's get going. Falling behind here and we don't need two kids fightin over a piece of pussy to hold us up none."

The men were milling about now, assuming their respective positions. Porter made an obscene gesture to Rowland with his groin and turned and went down the stairs to the sub-level of the rig.

"I'm goin to beat the breaks off of that son of a bitch," Rowland warned his uncle.

"Why don't you beat the breaks off this pipe," Les said. "Gummy, quit that. You know what I meant."

The floodlights flashed among the rig, and the last chink of chain sounded, the last break of tong, and the pipe lowered into the well. "That's it for tonight," Glenn called down to them. This is next shift's burden. Let's make like a turd and head out of this shit hole."

"I'm gonna get soused tonight, sure as shit," said Gummy.

Rowland made no reply. They walked.

"Listen, cousin," Gummy said. He stopped Rowland. "We see Porter tonight at Cal's Shade, and we'll get the prick together, okay? I ain't against a good old-fashioned ass kicking. In fact it's been too long, I need some excitement in my life again. We just can't have none of that here. I'd hate to see you get let go out of this place again."

Rowland watched his boot tips which were carapaced with mud. He nodded. Gummy patted his back and then they were moving again. Gummy hung an arm around Rowland's shoulders. "Let's just get good and drunk first, hear?"

They walked along the catwalk, their shadows on the ground below moving like drunken seneschals. Rowland thought about the poor soul before he again. "What caused that guy to get all ate up in the winch drum?"

Gummy hocked a string of dark phlegm over the rail. "Sandline snap. Cable come undone in wild wire, got the operator too in the back of the thigh. Liked to have took his leg off. He's mending up in the hospital still, the operator. The old one."

"Damn." Rowland shook his head.

"You should have seen all the commotion that done took place. OSHA investigated the matter for the better part of three months. Hell of a thing, it was. Been doin this for eight years and never have I ever seen a thing like that."

Inside the doghouse, Rowland punched out his timecard and sat at the little formica table, propped his feet up. "Smoke?" Rowland held out his pack of camels, Gummy slid one out, put it to his lips. Rowland flicked open and proffered a zippo. Gummy lit his cigarette and snapped shut the zippo and handed it back. They sat smoking without speaking. A deep violet dusk was filling the room. Rowland felt the pain in his side, promised himself it'd leave, but he knew it would always be back.

"Les," Gummy grunted. "When was the first well drilled here in the Permian?"

"I don't know, shit. Eighty-some-odd years ago?" Les said, looking out at the lights of the rig through the silted window and globbing thick copper-colored tobacco juice into his Pepsi bottle.

"Was you old as dirt then, too?" Rowland winked at gummy.

Les waved a hand at Rowland and grunted something.

"You're in a good mood," Rowland said, one bright eye asquint against the blue cigarette smoke curling ceilingward.

"Yeah. Why ain't you buggered off yet? You've known how to pitch a stick in my gears since before you could even crawl."

"Why ain't you gone on home yourself?" Rowland drew on his cigarette, turned his wrist and observed the smoldering cherry.

"Waitin on the other jackass toolpusher to get here. See his guys working? Where in the contumacious hell is he? He spat in the bottle. I'd like to know exactly that. The son of a bitch."

"Your crotchety ass needs to retire," Gummy said, working crescents of dark stuff from his nails with a pocketknife.

"I'll retire when I'm good and dead. No sooner."

They sought to their ablutions in the communal showers. Standing in the cheap plastic tube Rowland felt one of those spells come on again, felt his stomach turn on its axis. Nausea rocked through his gut like the surf of some awful sea. His jaw tingled, and he braced himself and vomited blood all down the side of the tube. His stomach contacting violently, his fists hammering the walls to regain his breath.

"Billy. Pardner. You doin all right?" Gummy

muted voice said from outside.

Rowland breathed deeply in his chest, his brisket very sore. "Yeah, bud," he said. He filled his palms with the falling water and splashed the blood off the sides of the tube, worked it down the drain with his feet.

The floodlights from the drilling rig cast tattered flags through the crazed workings of mesquite, black and iron-red vermiculated across the reticulate desert floor. While waiting for Gummy at his car, Rowland shucked out another cigarette and smoked, thinking about things. He thought about Mia. He remembered a dimly lit beer tavern. He was at the long mahogany bar drinking a bottle of beer. She'd been eyeing him the whole night. He remembered tilting the bottle back, her standing behind the bar, stretching over it to whisper something in his ear. The sweet speaking's from a soft palate. And watching while she did so the slip of red velvet garter in the bar back mirror and the immensity of pale white flesh cupped delicately under the hem of her little skirt. And then catching her watching him in the mirror, delicately biting her lower lip. They were the only occupants. They were like the last two survivors of Armageddon.

By now vehicles were filing out of the lot. He heard Porter's laugh sweep across the dusty dark, hanging among the sounds of industry and motor like the treble note of a bell tending off into a ghost chorus among other laughs like ancient ruins. And then he heard Porter's truck fire up, the rock steady cams growling in the earth. He remembered the time when he was only a boy, hunting the family hound pup that'd escaped the run when he'd come upon Porter and his father unloading bales of hay off the back of a flatbed truck on their own property. Rowland called for the pup, loping hind to fore in the sort of drunken dexterity young quadruped animals are known. He'd gone up the gravel path to the barn where the pup was and watched as Porter's father whistled the pup over to him. When the pup stopped, one hear slightly perked, its head cocked in a curious gesture, Porter's father climbed off the vehicle and took up his shotgun from the gun rack in the back seat and racked the slide and took aim and against Rowland's cries of protest, thumped a load of duckshot into the pup. He remembered it squalling horrifically, dragging itself, its jaws popping crazily at the air. But what he'd gotten in return to his curses hurled at them in nonsensical prolificness, were only laughs, mock tears. Then he heard another concussion and the pup's head broke open in the dust.

The progeny is always molded to the likeness of the sculptor. An old man told him that. And he thought him correct.

"Ready, cousin?" said Gummy, trudging among the shadows up to his car. Rowland answered and spun the cigarette falling in a long red arc and got in the passenger seat.

Their faces were stanched in green phosphorescence by the dash light. "Still keep that bottle hid under your seat?" Rowland asked.

Gummy did not answer, he just bent forward slightly, eyes fixed on the road, feeling the way a blind man might under the seat for it. His hand finally came up with a fifth of Early Times. "Here. But don't you go drinking it down and leave me with the dregs." He tossed it into Rowland's lap.

Rowland lifted it and unscrewed the cap and drank. "Shew," he said, coughing. "Stuff cuts your throat every time."

"Don't drink it all, shit," Gummy said. "I reserve that for them real rough days."

Rowland took another pull from the bottle and handed it back to Gummy. Gummy rested a wrist on the wheel and worked the cap off and took a drink. "When you goin to get that truck fixed up?" He asked through clenched teeth.

Rowland was watching the night race past the window. "When I've got the money," he said.

"What is wrong with it?"

"Got a crack in the block."

"Hairline?"

"Yeah. Transmission leak too. Among other things."

"We'll get her nice and right one of these days. Now that I think of it, we could just cannibalize a motor from one of my Chevy's—V-8 is what you got, right?"

"Yeah. V-8."

"There we go. Next weekend work?"

"Maybe."

"Just let me know. I'm always good for a beer or eight. And mechanicing, of course."

"Glenn says his brother drives with an outfit that hauls slaughter cows. Said it pays pretty well. Just need to get around to talkin to him about it some more."

Gummy laughed. "Well that didn't take no time at all."

"What do you mean?"

"Meaning you've only been back but a few weeks. Last time it was two, and the umpteen times before that ... Les ain't going to hire you again, I hope you know that. You need to know that."

Rowland got out a cigarette and lit it and pressed the little button to retract the window down the channel. "That's fine," he said. "I don't want to work drilling rigs all my life."

"Neither do I, cousin, but I suppose people in hell would like to have them a pair of ice skates. At some point you got to stop all this running and settle with something. No matter where you go, you leave when things is getting too tough. Ever time. Ever single time. It will be like that with that trucking gig, too. Just you watch."

Gummy swung the car to the right, and they rumbled over a cattle guard and slowed to a crawl in the caravan park. Rowland dropped the smoldering cigarette out the window, watching the trailer homes as they idled by. Gummy held the brake in front of Rowland's trailer house. Rowland noticed her car was missing. He thought about what Porter said and felt hot in his face. He thanked Gummy for the ride, and when he was climbing out, Gummy said, "I'll be back to get you in a hour tops. Gotta get the old lady fed fore she sets about a fit." Rowland nodded and lifted a palm in farewell and watched Gummy pull away into the night. He heard a clink of collar and a pit-bull climbed out from the bent and twisted skirting of the vacated trailer next door to greet him. Its tail nub moving excitedly, the dog squirming through his legs. "Hey dog," he said, squatting on his heels petting its neck.

Inside, he went to the refrigerator and got a can of Miller light and walked into the small front room and reclined in an EZ chair and turned on the television and sipped the beer. He thought of Porter laid up with Mia, their flesh touching. He hoped he would run into him at Cal's Shade.

After he'd come back from the refrigerator with a second beer, he saw the headlights of her car sweep between the slats of venetian blinds. He sat back down and pried the aluminum tab up with a thumb nail. Mia came in through the front door in heels bearing her cheap plastic purse. He noticed her standing, watching him from the door, but he did not say anything. He guessed he would wait for her to say something first. She did. She crossed into the front room and stood between him and the television. Her face all gaudy with makeup. He couldn't understand why he loved her anymore.

"Hospital bill come in," she said.

He thought she smelled of a whore.

"Not a hello, nothin?" He drank.

"Hello. We owe the hospital five grand."

"Let it go into collections," he said, leaning to one side so he could see the television. She sidled over to obstruct his view.

"Just let it go into collections? So it can affect our credit? How are we ever gonna get us a house? We won't never for that five grand, Billy."

"Won't effect our credit."

"I'm sure it won't. I'm sure you're just about as smart as you could be."

"Guy from work is goin to get me into trucking. I start in two weeks. Lot better pay, plus, I get to set my own hours."

"Great. So you'll be gone even more. Wonderful."

"Well, what do you want me to do? I see you're makin a awful lot with that whore money. Maybe I should slut myself out—"

She knocked his head askance. He ran a tongue between his teeth and lower lip, taste of metallic, like a canker. She stood over him, her bottom lip quivering.

"Get the fuck out of here," Rowland said.

She broke into a mute cry and spun away down the hall and into the bedroom. He heard the door slam. There was another slur of headlights through the blinds and then he heard Gummy's horn. Rowland got up and opened the front door, stuck an arm out with his index finger indicating a measure of time. "Be there in a minute," Rowland mouthed. He left the door ajar and ambled on down the hall to the bedroom. He tried the handle. "Can you unlock the door?"

Footsteps, handle click, the door opened. She stood with her hair all down her face like spilled ink. He could smell the caustic aroma of cocaine.

"I'm sorry," said Rowland.

She sniffled, ran a forefinger under her nose. "We just can't keep on this way. We can't do it."

Rowland propped his elbow against the jamb. "Is he still fuckin you?"

"Who?"

"You know who."

"Porter?"

"Yes. Porter."

"No."

"Are you lyin to me?"

"Yes."

Rowland dropped his arm at his side. "All right," he said.

Outside, the hot air pressed upon him a sensation of being cold, like an interminable fever, but it was not hot. The pit bull came up to him, a listless trot, tongue flapping uselessly from the corner of its mouth. "We'll see you, dog," he said, gently nudging it by with his boot. He opened the door, but before he could climb in, he was wrenched in his side with pain, pressed a palm hard into his flesh. He blew air through his lips, attempted to lose his thoughts with the sound of Creedence Clearwater blaring from the car's speakers.

"*You know I love you more,*" Gummy sang as Rowland slid into the seat. The pit-bull and other dogs down the street began barking.

"You are an asshole," Rowland said, pulling the door to.

"You're startin to sound like my wife." Gummy made a shuddering motion with his shoulders and put the car into gear and commenced to singing along with the tune again, cranking the volume knob up.

Inside Cal's Shade, Rowland nodded and shook hands with his coworkers through the smokey den of ball clack and beer clink and whoops of laughter. A local act was rehashing an Alan Jackson number in the corner. Guitars. Drums. Rowland could feel the music in his chest. The bar smelled like stale beer and drilling mud. It was a Friday night, a busy night. Some whores making their appointed rounds, holding cigarettes like little wands. But he had not seen Porter. He asked Glenn, and Glenn gave him a confused look. "Hey," he said, a hand on Rowland's shoulder. "I talked to my brother."

"Okay."

"He said he would hire you but thought the better of it on account of you bein ... bein a chicken shit." Glenn wheezed out a drunken laugh.

"I'm right here," Rowland said, brushing Glenn's hand off his shoulder. "So who's the real chicken shit?"

"I don't know, buddy. I like you—" he paused to burp. "—But you are sort of a big puss, excuse my french—a bitch, sorry."

Rowland patted Glenn's shoulder and left him tottering and went up to the bar. He ordered two Miller's in a bottle and found Gummy, who was speaking with a slattern looking country whore. "Hold on, darling babe," Gummy said to the woman. "I'll be with you right shortly." The woman smiled and clicked away on her heels. He turned to Rowland and nodded his head good-naturedly. Then he took the beer Rowland was proffering, and thanked him and said, "I guess Porter's lyin out his ass."

"I figured," Rowland said. "Glenn was giving me ten kinds of hell about being a bitch. I guess I'm a bitch tonight. I wondered why the guys were giving me funny looks."

"Apparently Porter told it to everybody that you was supposed to meet him in the parking lot. And apparently you did, and then left when he bowed up on you, and you kindly cowered off. What I hear."

Rowland shrugged. "Fuck it," he said, and tilted a drink down his throat.

"Whatever which way, cousin, let's get good and drunk. The hell with everyone. We're here to have a good time, goddammit. So a good time is what we're by God gonna have."

Rowland lost five dollars between two games of eight-ball and then excused himself for the men's room. He braced himself against the sink and huffed through the pain in his side. "Stop drinking, you dumb son of a bitch. Stop." He watched himself in the mirror, his face assumed a rictus of agony major. He couldn't even recognize himself these latter days. His face was hard in recollection; a face you try to build from dreams. When the pain went away, his attention had returned to Porter. He was probably at home with Mia. He was probably fucking her right now.

Stepping out of the men's room, there was a commotion among the crowd. He heard Glenn spouting invectives at Gummy at the bar. There was a sudden shift to the atmosphere of the room. The threat of violence was electrically charged, like the standing of hair before the strike of lightning. At the bar, a melee had erupted—stools and tables upturned in a crescendo, spreading toward Rowland like the concussive wave of an enormous detonation. Bottles went sailing like mortar fire, exploding on skulls, on walls. It was all out pandemonium. Gummy came pedaling backward out of the phalanx of brawlers and crashed up against the wall by the men's room. He turned to Rowland with a bloody, splay-toothed smile, assuming a classic pugilist's guard, and said, "I'm just getting warmed up," before getting sucked back into the fight. The guitarist for the band brought his guitar up over his head by the fretboard, and with a deft axman's grace, brought the instrument down over the head of someone grappling with someone else. Glenn was sweeping people off their feet with the backs of his fists like a movie monster while a small man dangled from his neck. He let the door to and started for the main entrance. Halfway there, someone hit him on the point of the chin and his head snapped like a band and he went down. He went the rest of the way on hands and knees along a floor murrhined with beer glass and legs of chairs with people tripping over him.

Just outside the door, a torpid redneck sat against the wall with his legs spread out before him like a child, a cigarette hanging from his lips. Rowland looked down. The man's eyes were dangling from their stems like a lobster and his head was all broken and the blood that pumped down his face looked like pine tar in that midnight hour. When he got to Gummy's car, Gummy was already behind it fighting someone. He had his fist wrenched in the collar of a man's shirt, and the man his, and they were punching each other in the face in a small-stepped carousel. Cars along the highway were honking here and there. Rowland walked up and fetched an overhand right at the man's forehead, and the man did a funny little pirouette, pitched, toppled over, and lay unconscious with his back on the hood of a neighboring car.

"He's a natural, ladies and gentlemen," cried Gummy.

Rowland held his bleeding hand and flexed it open and shut. "Let's get the hell out of here."

And then someone cracked him over the head with a pool cue, splintering it in two. He heard Gummy's voice slurring down a hallway. And turning to see his assailant, one knee buckled, and he doubled over. He heard everything in dreamy reiteration; the two of them, Gummy and the other man, scuffling in the gravel and cursing each other simultaneously. And then a curtain dropped over his eyes—his becoming world a dark beyond dark.

Rowland woke on cold concrete with his head swimming in a clabbered delirium. He eased himself onto his elbows and looked about. There was someone else sleeping on the floor and someone rocking and moaning into his arms on a concrete plinth that ran the length of one wall. Rowland turned onto his side, mashing his face into the crook of his arm.

Later they turned him into a cell with a leptosome man who was awaiting trial for murdering his family. "I really liked this gal," he said. "I think I truly loved this gal. I loved my little girl, I loved our little cats. I loved our house—our lovely, little house. And of course, I loved my wife. I would never deny that. There's just certain expectations a man should have, and sometimes you never realize how low you are, how sick you are, until something happens that's not rectifiable, that's all. Had I not been ordered to do so, I certainly wouldn't have murdered my entire family. And the cats."

"Christ," Rowland said and got up from the cot and walked out into the dayroom. He found an officer at a little station by a steel door. "Can I use one of the phones?"

The officer looked up at him. "Yeah, he said. Are you calling a lawyer?"

"No."

"Yeah. Yeah go ahead."

He went over to the wall of phones and called Mia. When she answered, he could hear her breath exploding into the receiver, gasps, moans. "Oh, oh," she went.

"Mia?"

"Hold on," she told someone. "What? Who is this?"

"Billy."

She was moaning again. "Oof," she said. It was quiet a minute. "Go fuck yourself Billy," she whispered, and the line went dead. Rowland scratched his eyebrow with a thumb. He couldn't help but laugh at the utter absurdity of the nature of that call.

There were a few numbers for bail bondsman plastered on the metal partitions along the wall of phones and he wanted to call one of them. But he was out of quarters. There was an inmate beside him talking on one of the phones. Rowland waited for the inmate to hang up and then rose and walked over to him.

"Hey, buddy," Rowland said. "My daughter is sick and I really need to speak with her, but I'm all out of quarters. Could I borrow one from you?"

"It ain't borrowing, motherfucker."

"All right. Can I have a quarter?"

"Shit man, what I look like to you? A fuckin charity?"

"Come on."

"Fine man, but don't ask me for no more shit."

The bondsman answered the phone. Rowland could tell he was a fat man by the way he breathed.

"I need to make bail, but I don't have any money," Rowland said into the phone.

"Okay. Name?"

"Billy."

"Last?"

"No, that's the first."

"No. Your last name. What is it?"

"Rowland."

"All right. Give me about a half hour and I'll be down to talk to you."

Forty-five minutes later the bondsman arrived and brought Rowland into a room. He was a big man indeed. Rosy cheeks, enormous gut looping over his belt. His slacks rolled up twice at the cuffs. "Here's the scoop, mister Rowland," the bondsman said. "If you ain't money for to make bail, then you're going to have to call someone who does."

"Okay," Rowland said, and gave him a number.

The bondsman was back in a few minutes. When he lumbered into the room, Rowland sat erect, attentive.

"Well," the bondsman began, slapping idly a clipboard against his enormous thigh. "That boy ain't posting bond his own self. He's in the next pod over for killing a man last night."

Rowland slunk defeatedly down the chair. So that's it for you, Gummy, huh? he thought.

His uncle Les was waiting for him in front of the jail in his maroon-colored Chevrolet Dually.

"Thanks," Rowland said, buckling his seatbelt. "Sorry you had to come get me."

Les rolled his jaw like a camel and spat into a bottle between his legs. He was clad in pinstriped night-ware. "You didn't make me do squat." He shifted the lever into drive and they took off.

It was quiet going for a while. Rowland watched his knees, listened to the drone of the diesel motor. He was nodding into dreams, but his uncle's voice woke him. "Heard about your pal Gummy? He called me right before you did."

"Yeah."

His uncle spat. "You guys give me hell about bein a teetotaler, but at least I ain't killed nobody. At least I had the nerve to quit. And you of all people, Billy, you've no right to be drinkin with what all you got going on, but who am I. Just your crotchety ass uncle. You'll see it one day, maybe. I hope."

They jolted over the cattle guard. Rowland was thinking of nothing at all. Les halted the truck in front of Rowland's trailer. "Before you get out, I want you to take a guess at how many of you wound up in jail tonight."

Rowland guessed.

His uncle held up five fingers. "Five," he said. "That's how many. That's five too goddamn many. Now get to bed. You've got to be at work in—" he glanced at the radio clock. "In four hours. Don't say nothin. Just get your ass out. I'll be by to get you."

Rowland nodded slightly, like a disciplined pupil, and opened the door and got out.

The pit-bull was standing under the light of the small porch waiting for him. "You've never waited for me up here, dog," he told it. It licked his fingers. He opened the door. "Come on in." It stood watching him with a cocked head. "Come in, idjit." The dog ambled in cautiously.

She had apparently moved out, Mia. The closet in the bedroom stood open and bare, some wire hangers strewn about the scurfed carpet. Her bedside lamp was still burning. As long as you didn't fuck him here, he told her pillow. He put something to cook on the stove—some slimy canned meat and fried it. Then he opened a cupboard and got two cans of green beans. He opened a pocketknife and punctured the tin lid and rocked the blade until he had space enough to pry the lid open with his fingers. He spilled one can into the pan with the crackling meatstuff and looked at the dog. "You hungry?" The dog looked at him, its tongue stropping its muzzle. "Can dogs eat green beans?" He fished a dirty bowl from the cairn of crockery in the sink basin and opened and upended the other can of green beans into it and set the bowl down on the linoleum and watched as the dog lapped it all up in about eight seconds flat. "Let's get you some more to eat. You like spam?"

He showered and lay sprawled under the sheets with the dog beside him on the floor. He twisted with agony, the tinge of copper riding his tongue, the cankerous taste of carrion. When the pain abated, he just lay listening to the dog breathing in the dark. He thought that perhaps he should feel something about Mia. He always thought if she left him, that he would be beside himself. But he guessed that in truth he hadn't loved her after all. He guessed he had simply grown comfortable and that the love he may have had for her died many years ago. But now, without her being here, everything was quite clear to him. It was dying. That's what he feared the most about her leaving. How many more months until your death? Four maybe? Five if the all powerful is generous?

Tomorrow after work he was going. He didn't know where to, but he guessed Florida was nice. But then again he'd always wanted to go to the commonwealth.

But he didn't wait. He was sitting on a duffel bag in the predawn dark at a gas station with his arms hooked around his knees and the dog curled asleep at his feet in the spits of rain when a car pulled up for him. He didn't even raise a hand.

"Get in," said the driver.

"Thank you," Rowland said, crawling in, the dog after. He closed the door, his duffel bag on his shoes. The dog sat panting, licked his hand. Then they were off. He watched out the glass, the liquid shapes of the town beading and trailing away from the window as they went. The world he was headed toward seemed infinite, uncharted. Out across the benevolent desert lands, the rain had slacked, the telephone poles were going, the distant wind turbines stood like sentinels under the gibbous moon. And over there run a parcel of deer. In their lunar castings their shadows keep another quadrant and these animals, loping, seemed imbued with a purpose antecedent to their origins. Both imperious and remote. Something divorced from their bosoms that was yet a blood constituent that transcends even you and I.

COMPANY OF AWFUL

The moment of my life I regret most.
 I once went out to a shack where my old girlfriend was holed up to get some amphetamines, but there was a problem.

She helloed me from where she was standing watering dead bougainvilleas in the front yard with a garden hose. She was wearing a dirty string-top and capris and was smoking a cigarette in her off hand.

"Daddy is feeling under the weather," she said. "He's got rabies."

"Rabies," I said. "I thought only dogs got rabies."

She smoked. "Me too."

"How'd he get rabies?"

"From our dog. From our little Pomeranian dog."

"Well where's the dog?"

"Over there. She gestured with her cigarette. In the woods over there."

I looked. There was a car wrecked into the trunk of this great big cottonwood tree. A little spire of black smoke rose up from the hood.

"Under the car?" I asked.

"No. Bobby tried to hit it, but it ran off."

"Oh," I said. "Shit. And your dad? Where's your

dad?"

"Bobby shot him," she said, and pulled on her cigarette.

"Who's Bobby?"

"Boyfriend." She moved the arc of water from the hose to another of the dead flowers.

"He killed him?"

"Didn't mean to. He's in the drawing room if you want to say hi."

"I thought you said he was dead."

"Bobby."

"Oh."

"Good to see you, Charlie. Been a long time." She spun her cigarette away and turned her attention to her watering.

"Yeah," I said. "Yeah."

So I went across the dead yard and knocked on the door of the dead-looking house where Nettie's dead dad lay. In a few minutes, Bobby opened the door. An adenoidal skeleton in a dirty wife-beater holding a machete. "Hey Charlie," he said.

"Hey," I said. "Nettie said you shot her dad."

"What the fuck else was I supposed to do? He had rabies. What the fuck."

"Can I come in?"

"Sure, yeah you can come in." He moved away to permit me entry.

The insides of this slattern shack of the damned smelled awful. I'd never actually gone inside before—I'd only been as far as the door, but as soon as I stepped in, I coughed up the caustic tang of bile. It smelled like death had been covenant with this place since Christ. He led me through trash and white dogshit to the drawing room. There was blood everywhere and a partially butchered human corpse. My insides folded on themselves.

"I need a little help," he informed me. "It's harder cutting through joints than I thought. Lot harder."

"Why are you cutting him up? Why not call the cops?" I couldn't help but fix my gaze on this mess, this ...

what words could you even use to describe it?

"Warrants, dude," he said. "I can't get arrested again. They'll keep me."

I was having difficulty following along with him. Having been withdrawing pretty bad—I'd kept getting these little brain zaps, as if my head had been opened up and this Bobby guy was poking around my brains with a hot wire. Anyhow, the matter at hand.

"I need you cut him up," he went on coolly and professionally. "I got guys coming to get rid of him, but he needs to be in bags, and in order to be in bags and transported correctly, he needs to be chopped up, you see?"

"I'm not cutting nobody up. Cut him up yourself. I just wanted some meth."

"He's got checks."

"What do you mean checks?"

"Some kind of government checks. The fucker had cancer."

"So he was going to die anyway," I said.

"Yeah. Of course. He was going to die anyway."

I regarded the bloody, half-butchered corpse laying on the floor. At this point I couldn't even smell anything anymore.

"Don't believe me," look at this. He produced his billfold and and withdrew three hundred dollars—crisp one-hundred-dollar bank notes. "Nettie cashed these this morning."

"What do I get out of it?"

"Some money. Some meth."

He was already dead.

I was just a junky.

I wanted to be liked.

So I picked up the machete and got to work.

COME NOT FORTH FROM THE DUST

Nayman was sitting in the booth by the window at the little café, watching the morning traffic accomplish itself, waiting for Lana. He ordered another cup of coffee, worked it down, and when he'd done eating his breakfast, he got up and paid at the counter, then stepped outside to smoke.

No sooner than he got a cigarette going did he see Lana's Pontiac downshifting for the turn into the lot. The bare metal spots of the roof catching and losing the sun in lustrous gleams. It was July, and early yet as the day was, the heat was already malefic. She swung the car up beside him and leaned and rolled down the passenger window. Nayman dropped his cigarette and toed it out like you'd squash an insect.

"Sorry," Lana said. "I had a hard time getting up and around."

Nayman nodded abstractedly, watching the cars along the road.

"Do you want to drive?" she asked. "I'm tired. I'm exhausted."

"Sure," he said. "I could drive."

He went around the front of the car and held the

door for her. When she climbed out, she wrapped her arms about his shoulders and kissed him.

"You ready?" he asked.

"I'm ready to get this over with."

They climbed in and Nayman pushed in the lighter on the dash and put the car in gear and they labored out of the lot, merging into traffic. She told him roughly where to go once they got to Wichita and said beyond that, that she didn't know the names of streets, but she knew how to get there. He studied her profile framed in the window by liquid light, studied the mauve bruise below her left eye. He thought about how much of a son of a bitch Enoch was for that. She noticed him watching and said, smiling: "I guess I won't bother asking whether you're happy to see me."

The lighter popped out and Nayman consulted his breast pocket for the cigarettes. He shook one out and lit it with the forge-orange coil and rolled the window glass down the rest of the way. He smoked, pulling on the cigarette thoughtfully. The tires making little slapping sounds at the cracks in the macadam.

"We ought to have just taken my truck," he said. "At least it has air conditioning."

"All you said you have to do is replace the compressor or something."

"It's not just replacing a compressor. It's a pain in the ass is what it is."

"If it was Carter Ann's car, you'd have done it. It would have been done and forgotten about by now."

"Well," he said, smoking. "She was my wife."

"Huh. Well. I just can't seem to wrap my head around why you'd want to come with me anyway."

Nayman grinned. "How about we turn on some music and just drive. How about we do that?"

He tuned the radio to the country music station and spun the dial way up. As he drove, he wandered his eyes intermittently from the road to the stencil-line countryside. Pastoral fields, windbreak trees falling away to virid blurs in their progress. Nayman flicked the cigarette out the window and relaxed in the seat. Lana found his hand on the center console, interlaced her fingers with his. He glanced over at her; the sun was caught in her strawberry-blonde hair like something alive. The same way the sun had caught her hair through the bay window where she sat watching Nayman hang drywall in her and Enoch's house those few months ago. Nayman thought about that for a while. She had cast some spell of Eros on him. They had been furtive in the beginning, or at least attempted it. But as time wore on, they left evidence in their wake the way a careless thief might, until the hammer came down hard upon Nayman when Carter Ann came home early from work and had caught them in the act on the living room sofa. She quit him then. And everything had fled from him in the smoldering aftermath. Wife, house, car. His infant daughter, Amy. Everything.

The house he'd then been reduced to was a squat aluminum house trailer with a jury-rigged room expansion, and when he'd first walked inside with the realtor lady there was still yellow caution tape up and the linoleum and subfloor cut out where a corpse had lain. Bullet holes pocked like the blossoms of small flowers along one wall. The windows with their glass shot out of their sashes, cardboard tacked up in their place for the weather. The realtor told him that someone had in fact died in that room. Something about the Sheriff's department, a meth lab, a shootout.

"Of course, we're a non-disclosure state," she had said. "But as you can see, the particular condition of this room might raise a few eyebrows."

"You said twelve thousand?"

"Yessir. Because it's a repossession we are only asking for the amount left on the loan. She leaned toward him and spoke quietly out of the corner of her mouth as though to keep from other ears but it was only the two of them. "Between me and you I don't know how the bank expects anyone to buy this nightmare. Would you want to raise a family where someone cooked meth and was shot and killed? I wouldn't, and I wouldn't blame you either. They just need to bulldoze this dump and take a match to it, but that's only my opinion."

"Will cash be all right?"

They were driving just outside of El Dorado, passing a sign that said: *Wichita 26 miles.* And stretched to the rim of the world, the iron pump-jacks rose and dipped like watering horses. The sky to the west was darkening, clouds wreathing dark underbellies until a huge canker flowered out of the mass and a loud clatter of thunder rolled like some great out of control stone careening down a corridor after them.

They pulled into a roadside filling station in the town of Benton. Nayman parked at a gas pump. They just sat there in the car for a minute. "Would you like anything? A drink?" Lana asked.

"I'm all right," Nayman said. She was getting out when he added: "Maybe some beer. Six pack of Miller."

He watched her cross the lot and through the pneumatic door. Then he got out and fed the pump his debit card and began to fill the tank. He drummed his fingers on the roof. He wondered about the future. Heat lightning relayed across the sky like a burning dossinia. When the handle clicked, he hung the pump nozzle up and got in the car and drove up to the door. Lana came out with a sack of beer and one of snacks. "They didn't have Miller," she said, pulling the door to. "But they had Budweiser."

"That's fine," Nayman said. "Hand me one, will you?"

"It's not even noon yet."

"Please."

She looked around cautiously and fished a hand into the sack and got out a bottle and reached it to him. He popped the lid off with the keys and drank a long drink and wedged it between his thighs.

"What if a cop sees you?" Lana said.

"Did anyone inside think I hit you?"

"Pardon?"

"It just looks bad. You being pregnant and that god awful bruise on your face."

"Yeah, and you drinking a beer in front of a gas station."

Nayman looked at her, at the small hump in her belly. "How far along did you say you are?"

"Twelve weeks. Somewhere around there."

Nayman tilted the bottle back and drank. Then he backed the car out of the parking slot and started for the highway.

Sitting on the tailgate of Nayman's truck in the front lawn earlier that week, Lana had told him how things had escalated with Enoch: In the kitchen they scrabbled at each other like feral cats in heat. Enoch's clenched fists assailing her in meaty whomps. She turned to make for the front door, but he wrenched a grip in her hair and whip-sawed her around and down onto the linoleum. She glanced up once with a frantic eye to see him straddle-legged over her and peering down at her wearing a look of crazed alacrity. She lay on her back screaming at him, flailing her arms about wildly and pedaling her feet in the air to thwart him off. Somehow amid the melee she'd managed to get her footing, and the fight bled into the living room. She got hold of a lamp and hurled it at him, her shoes. He shoved her hard through the screen door into the garage. She washed up against his workbench, slipped to her hands and knees, scrambled up again, her unsteady fawn legs keeping her from running, and horrified, wearing a classic mask of fear, to find that there were only the four walls and Enoch's boots crashing down the steps after her.

"That sorry son of a bitch," Nayman said. "You just need to get away from him."

"I did. Sort of. I had him thrown in jail over it."

There was silence between them, and they sat in it for a time. Nayman looked out past the ancient maple tree in its great wickerwork where little buttresses of light splayed through the enormous shade it cast. He sipped his beer. "So he found out about us," he said at length.

"Word spreads like the plague in a small town."

"How long will he be locked up for?"

"I don't know." She put her face in her hands. "However long it takes for his wino friends to put up the money to bond him out, I guess."

Nayman nodded slowly. "What did Enoch have to say? When the cops got there."

"Well, he started by saying: *I'm sorry Lana, it'll never happen again.* Then: *you're such a bitch Lana, you're a whore Lana*, as they crammed him into the back of the cruiser. She pushed her hair behind her ear with two fingers. I won't even think about dropping the charges."

"Get a no-contact order on him. That'll keep his ass away. Better yet, kick him out of the house. It's your house, too."

"But it's not."

"Your name isn't on the title? On anything?"

"No."

"Jesus Christ."

"I couldn't afford the house even if I wanted it. Not on my income alone. He's a big-shot in the oil fields. Or was. I don't know what's going to happen next. I just know that I'm leaving him when he gets out of jail."

Nayman drained his beer and pitched the bottle into the weeds. Dirt daubers rode the warm summer wind in a drowsy drone. He watched one land on the lip of the bottle and dance around the rim. Its thin yellow petiole bending like a willow switch as it tested its way inside. "Has he hit you before?" he said.

"Yes. But it's just the first time that it's been this bad. He's not all there, like mentally. He can't be. There was this one time, we were at the mall—store, whatever, and Enoch tells me that this guy looked at my ass in passing. I could already see his face turning hot as coals. I told him not to worry about it. People look. And he got real quiet. Didn't say anything else. Well, we get to the checkout lane, and he tells me that he's going to go pull the car up to the front. I say okay, and off he walks. I come out with the cart of groceries and he's sitting in front of the store with the car running. He gets out—by this time he's acting really sweet, talking to me, telling me that he's sorry for getting so upset and what all. He helps me load the groceries and then we leave. So I thought. We must have circled that damn parking lot at least eight or ten times before we finally left. And when we finally did leave, I noticed that he made the opposite turn we usually make to go home. Then I realized that we've been behind the same car for a good long while. Of course I ask what he's doing and he sort of disregards that and starts getting playful with me. At this point I know something is up. It just didn't occur to me quite then that what he was fixing to do was absolutely crazy. Anyway, we follow this car through a neighborhood. Now I'm getting quiet. I'm getting scared. The car in front of us pulls into the driveway of this house and Enoch pulls in right behind it. Then without saying a word, he gets out and goes up to that car and rips the guy right out of the seat and beats the living hell out of him. Right there in the driveway. The wife comes out screaming and then I see this little boy hiding behind her. He's seeing all of this. All of what Enoch is doing." Lana chewed sullenly on her lower lip. "I will never forget the look on that poor little boy's face. And I will never forget the horror in his eyes."

It had begun to rain and was raining yet when they passed the last grain mills looming, haunted-looking in the barren rainy murk, and joined with the toiling traffic at the edge of the city. Like the diurnal marching line of ants. Taillights progressed before them in red bleary whorls through the windshield. Water sluicing down the windows in staccato streaks. The wiper's steady arc cutting away the peening droplets. Lana told Nayman to take the exit here, and they went among a veritable warren of old houses, and Nayman thought to ask were they lost, but went along with her directions.

        He parked along the curb out front of the medical building. It was composed of Flemish brick and had a shake mansard roof. It sat wedged between houses, and Nayman speculated that at one time this too had been a house. Or perhaps still was. He didn't know. He looked at Lana. She was staring out through the wet window at the building, stroking the lunule of her jaw with one finger.

"Are you coming in with me?" she asked, reaching now into the backseat for an umbrella.

"I'm going to wait out here. This doesn't exactly scream the best part of town. And I'd hate for your car to get stolen and us left stranded in this circus show of a city."

"Well, okay," she said. "I shouldn't be long." She deployed the umbrella and shut the door.

He must have dozed to sleep for he jolted awake when she tapped at the window for him to unlock the door.

"How'd it go?" He asked dreamily.

"It went about as well as you'd expect for scheduling an abortion." She tossed her hair back and closed the umbrella. "Do you want to find someplace to eat?"

"I'm not hungry."

"Well, I sure am. I could eat a horse—hooves and all."

"How about The Beacon? Downtown. Got the chicken fried steak the way you like."

"Good enough for me," she said.

They had just got done eating and were waiting for the waitress to take the debit card when Lana said, "Did someone really die in your house?"

"Do what?"

"I thought you told me once that someone died in it."

"Yeah. Before it was my house."

"Well I know that. But is it really true?"

"What, did you not believe me the first time?"

"Never said that. It's just kind of peculiar is all."

"Here we are trying to eat a nice lunch."

"I think it's interesting, myself."

Nayman folded his hands together on top of the table. "You think I'm crazy."

"Maybe I'm just curious. Maybe I think you're a little crazy."

Nayman grinned.

"So it's true?"

"Yeah. It's true. Some kind of shootout or something. Dodge City style."

She nodded. "I wanted to be a crime scene investigator before I got into County dispatch."

"Why didn't you?"

"Ultimately there's just some deeply rooted personal things. Past trauma. Perhaps one day I could elaborate. I don't know." She pushed a piece of chicken fried steak around the plate with her fork. Nayman finished his glass of Coca Cola and studied the lunch goers.

"Do you think a thing like that ruins a house?" Lana said. "Someone dying in it? let alone getting killed?"

"I think people ruin places while living. But I suppose. I suppose an event like that stays in the walls forever."

"Do you believe in ghosts?"

Nayman smiled. "As in you think my house is haunted."

"Yes."

"No. I don't."

"You don't think there's such a thing?"

"I just don't think there's ghosts in my house."

"But what about events staying in the walls like you said. What is that supposed to mean then?"

"When you walk into a place where you know someone had died, you can feel it in the air. This sort of uneasy feeling. But what if you hadn't been told someone died. Would you feel it then? Could you tell?"

"Some may argue yes."

"They could be right. It's just something I'm not firm in believing. Maybe I'm a ghost. You could be talking to yourself right now and people are wondering what's up with this gal."

"You are crazy."

Nayman smiled.

The waitress came and got the card off the edge of the table and smiled at them and looked at the bruise on Lana's face with sidelong eyes and when she'd caught Nayman looking at her, she gave him a hatchet-lipped grin and walked away. Nayman made wet interlocking rings with the bottom of his drinking glass on the formica. He pursed his lips in thought. He could hear the clink of cutlery, cup clatter. Soft chatter. Then he looked up and saw Lana watching him affably. "Hold the fort," he said, rising out of the booth. "I need to use the men's room."

He went into a stall and got out his mobile and sat in his jeans on the commode. He flipped it open and thought about the number for a moment. Then he punched in the numbers. He sat waiting. It rang and rang. He ended the call and tried a different number. Finally, on the second ring, a man in Oklahoma picked up.

"Hello."

"Willy. It's Troy."

"I must be high as Giraffe pussy. Troy Nayman?"

"Yes."

"Hot damn. You here in Ardmore?"

"I'm still in Kansas. What have you got going on?"

"Hell Troy, God wouldn't be gracious enough to give me that kind of time. A lot has happened since you left. What, ass-crack of seven years ago?"

"I tried to call Carter Ann. Has she moved out of Oklahoma?"

It was quiet on the phone. After a while, Willy said, "Well, not really. She's moved closer to Eleanor, had her number changed."

"Moved closer to her mother? Is she living with her?"

"I said closer. But no. She ain't that ignorant. Eleanor's got cancer. That's how come."

"Do you have her number?"

"Who? Eleanor's?"

"Carter Ann's."

"Oh. Yeah, I do. But I don't reckon I could give it to you."

"Why couldn't you?"

"Why couldn't I? Because you ain't no good for her. I'm sorry, but it's the God's honest truth. What's happened is done and over with. I love you like a nephew, you know that. But I think you destroyed her life enough. With the drinkin and the drugs and affair and all. Shoot, right from the jump it was bad news. You two were pyrophoric as white phosphorus together. She's a month clean now. Quit the junk for good the day she drove down here. And I ain't no arbiter and I ain't whatever. It's just for the best. You need to understand that. So no, I couldn't give it to you."

"I just wanted to speak to her."

"You ain't got the sense God give a goose. Come drive down and speak to me. I'd love to have you here. I've got property in Springer now. A right pretty piece of land settin in the middle of nothin till it falls plum off the earth. Though I can't seem to understand how come I find spent condoms layin about. Damn teenagers'll try and cut the mustard anywhere, I reckon."

"Thank you for talking to me, Willy. But I've got to go. I'll be in touch."

He heard a labored sigh. "You really want to talk to her? I'll cut you a deal. She's goin through a lot right now with her momma. Just don't say some shit to make me regret it. You got somethin to write with?"

Nayman took out a napkin from his hip pocket and pressed it up against the partition. He had brought with him the pen the waitress had left at the table. He held the phone between his ear and shoulder and scribbled down the number. He hung up and dialed Carter Ann's new number. While it rang, his limbs went bloodless, and an entire marriage unreeled on the back of his eyelids. Vivid as a retinal burn. He wondered if Amy was talking now. Carter Ann recognized his voice almost instantaneously.

"I don't want to hear from you, Troy. Please. This year has been difficult enough. My mother is dying, and you are the last thing on earth that I want to deal with right now.

Nayman thought about her mother. Sickly, and on her deathbed. He remembered a different time, a younger visage. The harridan's claw raking across his face. The little pointed toe shoe cracking against the back of his skull.

"I was just thinking of you," Nayman said.

"Well, don't I just appreciate that. I'm sorry, but I've

really got more important things to do today."

"Are you still working the steps?"

"One day at a time."

"You looking for a sponsor?"

"Troy. I don't want to talk to you. Who even gave you my number?"

"Willy."

She made no reply. He heard her mother cough, small voices from a television set. Then he heard her say, "Troy." He sensed something to her voice, a lateral shift. What he took for an upending of the emotional axis. He thought that she might bequeath to him some form of forgiveness. I believe we can work this out, he imagined her saying.

"Yes?"

"Do not call this number again," and the connection was broken.

He watched her drive off with Amy down the winding driveway until the dust settled and the sound of the car was only a rumor of noise out there on the road. That dreary June morning. A moving truck was backed up to the porch with the roll up door open. Boxes stacked inside. Carter Ann's father came out through the front door passing Nayman, toting a heavy box down the porch steps. His name was Reese. Nayman watched him load the box into the truck silently. Reese dropped the door closed and latched it shut and swiped his hands across the seat of his slacks. He looked up at Nayman standing under the eaves of the porch watching him watch with baleful eyes.

"Let me tell you something," Reese said, propping one foot on the wooden porch steps, a hand on the porch rail. "I hadn't had the opportunity to speak to you much with my daughter and granddaughter still being here, but now that they've left, I can speak my piece. I hate you. I never did like you. But I was never going to tell my daughter who she can and can't be with. As a father to a grown woman, I can only express my concerns. That's all. The only good thing you've done is give me a granddaughter. And that's it. That's the pinnacle of your existence. That's all you have and will ever achieve in your godforsaken life—look at me when I'm talking to you—I wish they would have never let your ass out of rehab. Each day you were gone at Winfield I was a happy, happy man. I was happy because I knew my little girl was safe—same with my granddaughter. And to know that they were not in the maelstrom of some junky alcoholic got me some of the best sleep I'd ever had."

Nayman nodded solemnly at the warped boards of the porch. He had a cigarette hanging from his lower lip, one eye asquint against the curling blue smoke.

"Your daddy ever teach you to look a man in the eyes when he's talking to you?"

Nayman cut his eyes down at Reese. "I never knew him," he said. "He died before I was born. You know this."

Reese grinned good-naturedly. "I must have forgotten. They say addiction runs like syrup in the blood."

"You go to hell," Nayman said.

"Naw. I know who my maker is."

Reese studied this reprobate before him. His jaw knotted, relaxed as if in chewing, but he was not chewing. He sucked his teeth and stood erect. "You've got a cold front moving in on your neck with that Enoch boy."

Nayman spun his cigarette away into the weeds. He looked at him. "I'm not worried about him," he said.

"You should be. I've had to represent him in court before. You know what he was in court over? It wasn't over not paying a speeding ticket. No. He was in court because he took a lug wrench to his brother's head. Normally on account of that, you could just chalk it up as self-defense, something of that nature. Something somewhat understandable. Something with a foothold in the court of law. But Enoch's case wasn't in self-defense at all. It wasn't over anything really. How can you knock your own brother in the head with a wrench over a game of cards and not give it any more thought than someone throwing away trash? Enoch himself couldn't even tell me why, and I was his appointed attorney. Those details matter. You have to have something to build a defense with. Truth is he didn't give a shit. I'd asked him the day of the trial what he would have done differently if he could go back in time, and he looked me square in the eyes and said he'd have hit the cheating bitch twice as hard. That's the kind of animal that you're up against here, and the odds are not in your favor." Reese grinned a wide toothed grin. "Just imagine what he'd do—what he will do—to someone sleeping around with his wife." He opened the door to the truck. He had one foot in and turned to look at Nayman a final time. He said, "So my best advice to you, old buddy, is to get the fuck out of El Dorado. You've done notarized your very own death warrant."

At a quarter after two they were back in El Dorado. Lana rolled into the parking lot of the cafe in which she'd picked up Nayman earlier that day and parked beside his truck to let him out. Bob Dylan was singing lowly on the radio. Nayman's hand was hanging from the grab handle by the window, and he was studying his truck over his arm. "You got anything else to do today?" he said.

"Not really, no. I was just probably going to head home and do a whole lot of nothing. Maybe sleep."

"Mind if I swing by your place? I was thinking about replacing that compressor."

"Just remember. It's the third right."

"I thought it's the second."

"You think that because you always miss the damn turn."

"Hell, they all look alike."

"Right. Nothing more confusing than an absolutely flat as flat can be countryside with only a few windbreaks."

"So, third from the first turn?"

"Would you get the hell out of my damn car."

The front door swung open and Lana came outside bearing two glasses of sweet tea over ice. The small cubes clinking delicately within the glasses as she went. Nayman slammed the hood shut and lit a cigarette, one thumb hooked through his belt. He was wet through with sweat.

"That didn't take all that long," said Lana, proffering one of the glasses to him. "I thought you said it would be a pain in the ass."

He took the glass of tea and drank huge gulps from it. His throat working it down rapidly. It was cold and very good. He drained the glass and crunched the little mint leaf with his teeth. "I just didn't want to do it," he said, wiping his mouth with the back of his hand.

Lana smiled. She leaned her hips against the front quarter panel and drank. "What changed your mind?"

"There was this little gnat kept buzzing in my ear. It would quit for a while and then buzz buzz it would come again."

She slapped his shoulder. "You turd."

"Fire her up and see if she farts some cold air at you." He stomped out his cigarette. "Here I'll hold your glass."

It did. She sat for a moment with her eyes closed and the motor chugging. Just taking it all in. Then she smiled and cut the engine and crawled out and took her glass from him. "Oh my God, that feels so nice."

"Happy?"

"More than. Thank you."

Nayman cast his eyes to the pasturelands beyond her. He saw distant ranged cattle wavering and slearing under the weight of the sun. Birds in the sky. "What do you want to do?" he said.

Lana brushed her hair behind her ear. She gave him a funny little half-smile. "What do you want to do?"

He woke splayed overtop the sheets of her bed with her head on his chest and her breasts pooled like wax against his ribs. He eased away from her and threw his legs over the edge of the mattress and just sat listening to the ceiling fan. He saw a nickel plated .38 revolver on Enoch's bedside table and picked it up. He pressed the cylinder release and opened up the cylinder and spun it slowly with his thumb, counting the brass cartridges in each chamber. He closed the cylinder and put the pistol back and looked behind him to where Lana was sleeping. Then he got up and dressed and swept the revolver off the bedside table and shoved it in his belt and went down the hall.

He passed through a curtained doorway into the living room. A wide wall of light falling slant from the skylight where motes or flecks of dust hung gold and trembling in the midafternoon sun. A tall mahogany case clock stood along the far wall by the kitchen with a brass pendulum swaying slowly behind its casement door. There was a picture table by the back door and he saw in a gilt frame a photograph of Lana and Enoch in some small boat on a lake. He picked it up and looked at it. Enoch's head was cocked back in guffaw and Lana had her head on his shoulder and a hand at his belly. Nayman trailed a finger down the length of her thigh.

"Troy?" said Lana.

He set the picture back on the table and turned around. "You two look real happy here," he said.

She had a robe on and was coming forward with her arms folded under her bosom. That was a long time ago, she said. Then she sat down on the arm of a sofa and crossed her legs. He looked at her with his hands shoved in his pockets.

"You wish you hadn't come here," she said.

"No, it's not that."

"Then what is it?"

"I don't know. We've just made a lot of bad decisions together."

Lana picked at her lower lip. "Is it the baby? Do you want me to keep the baby?"

"And if Enoch finds out?"

"He knows I'm pregnant."

"I'm talking about after the baby is born. He's going to know it's not his."

"He already knows it's not his. That's another reason why I'm terrified about him getting out."

"You told him."

"I had no other choice."

"Bullshit."

Her face was wet. "What was I supposed to do? It's not his baby and God knows what would happen if he found out later on. I had to. You even said yourself that it wouldn't be a great idea to keep it."

"I say a lot of dumb shit."

"Then we can keep it. Believe me, I'd love to keep it. I'd love nothing more than to keep it."

"Okay."

"Okay."

"Then we keep it."

She wiped her tears away. "So what do we do? If we decide to go through with this pregnancy, then how do we get out of this situation?"

"I don't know."

"What do you mean *you don't know*."

"I mean I don't know. I don't know what the hell we do."

They heard what sounded like a car pull up to the house. The first thought Nayman had was: Enoch. They stared at each other for a minute. Nayman could feel his heart hammering his eardrums. Then a knock at the door. Another. It was quiet in the room. He could hear the clock ticking. Finally, Lana started to rise but Nayman said, "I'll get it."

He crossed the room and parted the curtains of the picture window overlooking the front lawn but from this position all he could see was a rear chrome bumper turning back the sun like a heliograph. He could feel the gun in the small of his back. He went to the door and poised his hand over the knob and then took a breath and opened it quickly. A short fat man in a tan summer suit with a pamphlet doffed his hat. "Good afternoon, mister. Today—yes that's right, today—"

Nayman slapped the door shut.

"Who was that?"

"Some guy with a pamphlet."

He hoped that maybe he wouldn't see her for a while. He'd found some semblance of peace in his life again, what little there was. He last saw her on Friday and spent the weekend working little jobs by day and spending long nights at the Blue Goose tavern, drinking whiskey neats and shooting pool. Chatting up the young things. But then there was Enoch. Everywhere he looked he saw him. He was still in that jackpot and he knew he'd be in that jackpot until something put a stop to it. But he didn't know what that something might be. He didn't want the phone to ring and he didn't want her car to pull into his driveway and he didn't want to think about the baby. He didn't want to think about her at all.

When Willy called with the news, Nayman was running the last bead of caulking on a pair of double hung windows that had taken him all day to complete because a demented codger kept accosting him from the street and calling the cops on this midday home invader. He couldn't wait to get the hell out of there. He stood down off the ladder and answered the call.

"You settin down?" Willy asked.

"Why, what's going on?"

"This ain't somethin I want to do at all, Troy. I've been dreadin this call. I've been goddamn dreadin it."

"Willy. Who died?"

"Well, Carter Ann was headed back from the grocery store and..."

"Yeah?"

"And she was involved in a wreck. And it ain't lookin good."

Nayman could hear Willy fighting back his tears. "And Amy," he said. "Oh God—I don't know no better way to put this, but Amy, she didn't make it to the hospital."

Nayman rested an elbow on a ladder rung and pressed a fist to his forehead. He was in utter disbelief. He mouthed how to say a word but remained silent.

"I need you to say somethin here," Willy said.

"She's dead," Nayman said perhaps only to himself.
"I'm sorry bud. I'm so sorry."

Nayman blew air out of his nose and closed his eyes. "They found drug paraphernalia in the car—in

Carter Ann's. Don't take my word as bible and verse, but they is reason to believe that Carter Ann was back on that junk. That heroin whatever. If her blood work comes back hot, and if she pulls through this, she's goin to be in a shitpot of trouble."

"What did they do with Amy's body?"

"What?"

"Where did they put Amy's body?"

"Come on man. I believe she's in the morgue. Let's not talk about that."

"Are you in Oklahoma City?"

"Yes."

"Which hospital?"

"Mercy. But don't come down today, Troy, I'm beggin you. Reese is bad off mad at you and I just don't want nothin to go sour. Emotions need to simmer first."

"I want to see Amy."

"They won't let you—not yet anyhow. Please Troy. They didn't want you to know but that's your little girl, and even after all the hell that went on, that's your ex-wife too. You needed to know."

"Who didn't want me to know?"

"I'm talkin too much."

"Who didn't want me to know."

"Reese."

"Kiss my ass," said Nayman. He pinched the bridge of his nose between his thumb and forefinger. "When did this happen? Today?"

"On Saturday."

"On Saturday? And you're just telling me now?"

"You've got to understand…"

Nayman folded the phone shut. He muttered curses to himself and put his hands on his hips and worked his jaw open and shut. Then after a time he commenced to packing away his tools. He didn't know what to do with himself.

"How would you like it if I called the cops on your young ass? Put that ladder back where you found it," the old man in sockfeet cried out from down the street. He was wearing only jockey shorts and a stained and tattered tank top. "I will call them, you filthy thief. Don't think I won't."

Nayman stood with the door to his truck open. "Call them," he said.

At dusk he arrived in Oklahoma City. He parked in front of the hospital and waited and cried but could not compel himself to go inside. He came back later with a fifth of whiskey drank down to a third in his lap and put it in the glove box and got out drunkenly and went inside the hospital. He'd asked around and a nurse in the hallway told him what room she was in. As he was coming out of the elevator, he saw Reese and Eleanor with a walker and oxygen tank standing in wait. Nayman told them that he was sorry and expected them to order him to leave. But they did not. Instead, Reese just gave him a cold level look and said nothing and helped Carter Ann's mother into the elevator.

He pulled up a chair next to the bed and sat with his elbows on his knees and his hands folded together. He studied her laying there. All those cords, tubes, wires. The machine breathing for her with pneumatic hisses. It was cold, so cold in there. The air smelled of disinfectant and of sickness. Although she in all probability could not hear him, he told her that he was so sorry and that he loved her. He said a prayer even though he himself was not religious and then a nurse came in and told him that he needed to leave.

When he drove into the city limits of El Dorado he stopped by an ATM and withdrew three one-hundred-dollar notes and drove to the Autumn Acres trailer park to visit an old friend with death very much on his mind.

He'd no idea what hour it was or for how long the knocks at the door had been coming, but he finally woke to a voice commanding him to open the door. He lay on the cold, buckled linoleum floor of his living room in a welter of sweat. He clambered to his feet and on unsteady legs, tottered to the door with a palm held to his forehead. He eyed the judas-hole and saw Reese's stretched face.

When Nayman opened the door Reese immediately

charged into the foyer and took hold of Nayman by the collar of his sweat-soaked shirt with both hands and wept, becrazed with fury and heartbreak, and yelling through his clenched teeth unintelligible mutterings. They went to the floor, Reese atop of him, his fists still balled up in Nayman's shirt. Nayman peered into the eyes of this grieving patriarch above him. In the rims of those eyes where tears boiled and ran, he saw dead leaves shifting and then scudding, saw rafts of sleet snow trailing in a cold bitter wind; and lastly, he saw the cognate soul of a wounded man for a thousand sufferings to come.

"You took everything away from me," Reese said, letting go his grasp and sitting erect, his breath exploding, voice trembling.

Nayman felt the room whorling like the print of an enormous finger. He was overcome with nausea. "You're not the only one hurting here, Reese," he said, propping up on an elbow. "I lost my little girl for Christ's sake."

"She wouldn't have ever picked up a needle in her life if it wasn't for you. You pulled her world apart with that fucking affair and she goes and does what you trained her to do. To jam a fucking needle in her veins."

"I didn't train her to do anything."

"Shut up. Just you shut the hell up."

They sat breathing heavily and not talking and the house was quiet otherwise. Reese stuck a leg up and piled his hands over his knee and pushed himself standing. His black tweed suit was all disheveled and his necktie loose and bunny-eared. "You're high right now, aren't you, you little prick," he said, adjusting his tie.

Nayman did not answer. He could feel his stomach turn. Vomit crept up the back of his throat. He gagged it down. Reese passed a thumb below his nostrils and shook his head at the entirety of the situation. At the weight of it. He looked around the little room and pressed the back of his wrist to his mouth and sobbed briefly. Then he wiped his mouth with his fore knuckle and looked down at Nayman. "I'll be damned all the way to hell if I catch your ass anywhere near the funeral," he said, and left Nayman where he lay.

It rained for four days. It rained and he couldn't work and it rained. For two days he sat drinking Wild Turkey and watching the rain fan opaquely from the wonky gutter. On the third day he got in his truck and drove to Lana's house. He'd begrudgingly gone, not out of the want of doing so, but in finding that she filled some tenantless place within him that he'd not even been made aware of. Lana had always said that she loved the rain. She'd said that it brings her some serene feeling that was not unlike pure tranquility. Nayman thought her swollen belly had grown although it had only been a week since he'd been with her last. He told her about Carter Ann and about Amy and she consoled him and he did not want to cry but he could not help himself and he wept perhaps harder than he ever had than when he was alone. They made love and talked about life and they talked about the future. Lana had called the county corrections facility—twice that he'd actually heard—inquiring of Enoch's detention status.

For the first time since the beginning of the affair she had told him of her girlhood. They were sitting on a slat board bench on the back deck watching the rain. Nayman was drinking a beer and she was sitting beside him with her legs tucked under her drinking a cup of tea. She told him that she was born in Japan. At Yokota Air Force base, she said. She was a military brat, grew up all over the states. She said that when her father got out of the service they settled in El Dorado to be close with his side of the family. Her grandfather had dementia then and none of her aunts nor uncles would offer any clemency for his condition. She said that they just wanted to stuff him away in some home. But that her father took care of him until he ultimately died.

"My father was a great man," she said. "He really cared about us. But the same couldn't have been applied to my mother. Us kids could tell that his heart wasn't in it. So after putting up with all the fighting and bickering my mother had finally decided that she couldn't do it anymore and filed for a divorce. They weren't married but a few years. My father said okay, just like that, and they got divorced. She never went after money or anything like that. They just cut ties amicably and did a wonderful job coparenting."

Nayman sipped his beer. Lana drank her tea and talked at the falling rain as if she were addressing it. "Can I tell you a little story about what came of my mother, and you tell me if you can spot the iceberg implications of it?"

"Iceberg implications. Sure," said Nayman.

"My mother died pretty young. Had me pretty young too. Sixteen. All my brothers and sisters came from my father in a previous marriage. He was significantly older than her, my mother. Anyway, she had a rough, terrible childhood and I think after the divorce it gave her time to dwell on that. She started seeing this shrink, this psychiatrist, to help cope with her past experiences. Well, she ended up falling in love with him and he with her, shockingly enough. My mother wound up pregnant and they got a shotgun wedding done. They bought a house together, started getting the nursery ready. All of that. But she miscarried my baby sister and her husband wound up getting drunk and crashed his car into an abutment on his way home that night and died. That very same night. You can imagine how much that might affect someone. She wound up taking some combination of pills later on and it killed her. She didn't want it to look like a suicide, God bless her soul, but it was. It was. Us kids got together and had her buried in her hometown—in Anadarko Oklahoma. We got the money together to have her buried in this granite mausoleum. It was big and so beautiful. Then somebody broke into it and her body went missing."

Nayman looked at her.

"We got the police involved and what happened next took us all by complete surprise. It turns out they found her body three-hundred and fifty miles away in this taxidermist's house in Dogpatch Arkansas and he was living with her corpse for several months. Not just living with her but trying to preserve her. Had all these strange chemicals and stuff. Even had most of her corpse stuffed. And get this, he had a number of different dresses for her and everything—makeup. And disturbingly enough, they found used condoms in a waste basket by the table he had her on. Believe it or not the police had actually found my mother by coincidence. They had originally gone to his house on suspicion of a different crime but the smell that wafted through the door had them concerned and very much curious. He tried to play it off as doing work from home, whatever that could be, but the police didn't buy it, as you could guess. They said that the taxidermist himself smelled like he'd been embalmed. They ended up leaving and returned to his house before the ink on the warrant had dried and arrested him."

"Good God," said Nayman. He turned the bottle in his hand and shook his head.

"He simply didn't want to let her go. I don't know where he ended up. Whether it was the penitentiary or the madhouse, I don't know. We had the body delivered back to Kansas and my grandmother had her cremated here in El Dorado."

Nayman didn't say anything. He drank his beer.

"Do you see?"

"I don't know, he said. I don't know what you're trying to get at."

"I told you that because that's what I want. I want someone that will abandon all principles and say to hell with the world and love you no matter what and absolutely nothing could stand to prove otherwise. Including the grave."

As told it rained on the fourth day. Nayman drove to a filling station and bought a slice of pizza and a coke and ate in his truck with the rain stringing down the windows. When he'd done and had asked himself if he were ready and then answered no, he got out and went to the payphone on the corner. There were three funeral parlors in town and when he'd dialed the second funeral parlor from the directory, a young man spoke to him.

"Is there a Nayman funeral that had already happened or will be taking place? The Amy Nayman funeral?"

"Yessir. The burial will be at one-thirty this afternoon, sir."

The *Amy Nayman* funeral. Hearing those words spoken aloud so disoriented him that he put his head in his forearm over the phone's housing.

"Sir?"

"Which cemetery is the burial to be?"

"At Belle Vista, sir."

"I appreciate it."

He parked across the street from the Kansas Oil Museum and walked with his shoulders bunched for the rain through the wet grassy fields and went into a dripping wood and followed the course of a winding creek before coming at last out onto a rail spur. Here he crossed the tracks and went uphill along a rain chewed gravel road. Then he stopped when he'd seen them among the menhirs. Reese, Eleanor, Willy. Other mourners he'd not seen before or could not put names to. Children. They were all veiled in black and standing under umbrellas or under the big green canopy listening to the preacher who was standing beside the tiny casket wherein lay his lost progeny. He went up a short way into the grass and leaned his back against a telephone pole. They did not notice him standing there. He could not hear anything. He was completely wet through to the flesh. His socks were soaked in his shoes. Then after a while the preacher shut the Bible and held it by the spine with both hands at his waist and the mourners rose and each in turn set flowers on the casket and each in turn began to cry. Then the straps began to lower the little casket into the earth and Nayman now too began to cry. Elenor crouched with her walker and oxygen tank sobbed hysterically, her cries carrying across the stones like those cries so fabled by mariners of old. Nayman turned to leave. Peering back once to see Willy raise a hand hello. Nayman raised his slightly and dropped his head and started back down the hill, wrenched in his heart by an agony heretofore never known to him.

She was waiting for him when he got home. When he met her on the porch he could see in her countenance that she was frightened, troubled, something. "He's out," she said. "He's either out or getting out. I called the jail and they told me that he'd posted bond. Somebody put up the money."

"Well, he can't touch you. Or I for that matter. He doesn't have enough fingers on both hands to count the number of charges he'd catch."

She was shaking her head. "You should know by now that he doesn't give two shits. None of that matters to him. He's pissed."

"Do you think he'd come home right away?"

"That's what I don't know."

"How about you go pack an overnight bag? You can stay here tonight, and we'll work something out later. I'll go with you."

"No. I will go alone. I don't want him to walk in and see us together."

Nayman pecked a cigarette from his pack and lit it. He watched her pace about the porch.

"I'm going to give him an ultimatum," she said. "That's what I'm going to do. I'm going to talk to him and tell him that I will drop the charges if he simply gives me a divorce. Maybe he can find reason in that."

Nayman pulled on the cigarette. "And if that doesn't work?"

"I don't know. I will try and find a way to call if everything went okay. But if I don't call—if you don't hear from me, please, Nayman, get to my house."

He watched the ceiling light play in the contents of his beer bottle. Like chemicals in a beaker glass. If he saw portents there it was much the same. He waited for his phone to ring but it never rang. And after the gauzy sun had dropped to its last recrements of day, so then came night to its ultimate endarkment. His mind was made up. He rose from the EZ chair drunkenly and walked to his bedroom. He got Enoch's revolver from underneath his pillow and stood, listing slightly, with it in his hands. He wouldn't actually use the damn thing, but he figured if worse came to worst he could threaten Enoch with it if in the case that he was on top of her.

He sat in his truck with the revolver on his lap. He called Lana twice but each time all he heard was her voice after the dial tone. He knew that she was in trouble. He put the revolver under the seat and stuck the key in the ignition and started the truck. Then he switched on the headlights and backed up and pulled away, the car pitching and swerving drunkenly down the rain guttered gravel drive.

There were no lights on at her house. Just the house itself augmenting up out of the rain and the dark in the yellow nimbus of Nayman's headlights. He put the car in park and cut the lights and the engine. The rain drummed on the steel roof. The wipers raked across the windshield. He looked at the house. The black windowpanes wherein whose darkness he knew not what lay. Who might lay. He reached into the glove box and fished out the bottle of whiskey he'd kept hid there and unscrewed the cap and drank and when he'd finished the bottle he reached under the seat and got the revolver and climbed out.

He ascended the porch steps, slipping once belligerently, and tried the door but it was locked. He called Lana's name and lambasted the door with the hilt of the gun. He waited. Nothing, rain, silence.

His boots sucked in the mud as he slogged, staggering his way to the rear of the house to the back sliding glass door. He stamped his shoes on the boards of the deck to free the mud from them. The world was rocking in a nauseating centrifuge. When he tried the handle the felt weatherstripping popped. He waited. Then he slid the door open and stepped inside. There was only the palest of light thrown across the floor from the gaps in the drawn curtains of the window across the room, but other than that was darkness entire. He stood swaying. There was something that he could not name that felt wholly out of plumb. He thought he should hear the case clock ticking. Then in a drunk's transient clarity it hit him like a stake in the gut. "You jackass," he said. "It's the third turn. It's always been the third turn."

The crack of the bullet when it came bequeathed him (and occurring almost instantly from dark to sourceless dark) an outrageous clamor with just the faintest muzzle flash like the   ensparkment of steel on stone that snapped at his chest and withdrew in absolute finality back into the increate universe from which it came. Nayman fell backward, cracking the back of his skull against the tiled floor. The revolver went clattering across the tile. The glass of the door webbed and then detonated in a shimmering waterfall. A red boutonniere bloomed from his breast and he could feel hot blood tracking down the sides of his rib cage. He didn't feel anything. He lay with rattled breath and closed his eyes. *See a light, a green gas sun shunting down dark and mucoid architraves. Somas with their myelin sheaths eddied and were sucked away. Nayman now barreling down along a galactic string; past Canis Major, Cassiopeia. He could hear a whining castor from some wonky cart. Schizoid voices in a cosmic comedy. Lights passing and repassing over his closed lids like strobes through a patagium.*

See now atavistic kinsman in kaleidoscopic parallax like ghosts behind colorplate glass. His footfalls exploding in a cistern. The figures shifting to see this limboed dipsomaniac threading his way through the shadow show. And then he saw her. Here before him lies Amy in a liveried cradle on a platform among the watchers, among the dead. Among the faceless enterprise of the forgotten in whose very names were ash and legend.

"Yeah, I've got them on the phone," a woman's voice cried from upstairs. "Did you get him?"

"I hit the son of a bitch," a man said.

The lights came on. An old man in cotton nightwear held a pistol leveled at Nayman with one hand, the other falling away from the wall switch. "Make sure you let them know the crazy bastard's got a gun too," he said.

ABLUTIONS

Dear James,
    To catch you up to speed, this past year has whipped my ass sincerely. I've been shot at, stabbed twice, once for each separate occasion, overdosed a couple of times, died, revived, treatment facilities twice, and so on. All those adventures landed me in the El Paso County lockup, where I'm sitting, right now, in my cell, giving you a little ink. Yep, the doctor is canned, all within this year. By the way, the blue work shirts and denim pants and moccasins they make you wear in here aren't all that uncomfortable in truth. And they feed you cigarettes. Food is about what you'd expect. I also heard Jane Fonda was up in Northern Vietnam in I think, July? Please tell me you got a picture with her. Anyway James, get out your fork.
    As you know, I began the year going to an anesthesiology residency up in Albuquerque. Long hours. Sometimes over twenty-hour shifts, depending on whether there was a surgical operation or not. To get through those shifts I began taking pharmaceutical speed—black beauties, what they call it. That shit would make you chew your lips off, and if you were lucky your gums would bleed. I only did black beauties a handful of times, and that was it. My fate was

sealed. That was the beginning of the end, friendo. I wish that it all stopped there, but hang on, it gets worse.

You wouldn't believe how many anesthesiologists try out different drugs on the job. A lot. It's just too tempting. The most common drug is Fentanyl, a narcotic anesthetic that was relatively new to the hospital in which I was completing my residency in. I saw how wonderful the Fentanyl made patients feel. Their frayed moons mended. Their souls on rafts of lavender clouds. I began using it intravenously. Getting the stuff was easy. All I had to do was open up a cabinet door and take as much as I needed. And I'd take a tourniquet and syringe into the men's room, or the OR suite, and junk the stuff into my veins. Then get up, and go back into surgery with a warm, buzzing mind. But of course I didn't have a problem. No, no, I can handle this, I'm not an addict. Dope-heads are only in the papers or television programs, they aren't doctors! But Joe, they absolutely are. I got away with copping Fentanyl for a couple of months. And then I really started to swim in my own poisoned blood.

Once, during a twenty-four-hour craniotomy operation—brain tumor removal—my relief would hit about every two hours on the nose. I'd run to the OR suite and get my fix of Fentanyl. But later on, during the operation, my relief didn't hit. The procedure was going south, and the patient at this point was losing a lot of blood. Because I was beginning to experience withdrawals, I became distracted, my thoughts zoomed. Those important connections in my own brain were misfiring and I lost focus. I injected a blood product into the wrong port of a catheter, resulting in the patient developing a blood clot that travelled to her right lower lung, and she, by medical definition, arrested. We began to panic. We did everything we could to work her out of death; Bicarbonate, Adrenaline, and a few other things of which I cannot remember. But it was the defibrillator pads that restored her life. To this day I think she still has a palsied face, and I see it on the back of my eyelids at night, every night. Just a friendly reminder.

But that's the thing, sometimes people arrest during an operation for no evident reason. It just happens like that.

No one realized my mistake had caused her arrest, and the unfortunate aftermath she will have to deal with for the rest of her life. But it was because of me, I have to accept that.

Heroin was my next love affair. It was easy to get too. If I ran dry on my supply, I'd double up the dosage of narcotics for a patient, and give said patient only half, and keep the rest. I even had a few orderlies I was dating at the time write me prescriptions for hydrocodone, also a narcotic. I never got questioned, never accused. Who accuses a doctor of a drug problem?

Every morning I'd carry with me six or twelve twenty-dollar baggies of heroin to the men's room in the hospital. And before my shift was up, I'd have the cold sweats and vomit into the sink. I was getting sicker, James, and I knew it. I was making close to a six-figure salary and I couldn't even afford toilet paper to wipe my own ass with because it took 300 dollars a day to get high. When I quit getting high from heroin, it cost me 300 dollars a day just so I wouldn't take ill and feel like a parasite were eating my bones. I had all the stressors every doctor can have—anxiety, pressure, etcetera, etcetera. Everything doctors put up with, which they take drugs to relieve. But in my such case, those listed reasons were not my excuse. I took drugs because I loved taking drugs. *Loved* them! They made me feel like God!

James, my insides were dissolving into mud. It felt like my veins were all scratched up and scurfy. I'd shoot up twenty, thirty times a day. My mind was disintegrating, man. I'd wore out all the veins in my arms and legs, so I began shooting up in my neck. You think you're clever in that state, wearing long sleeve shirts and turtlenecks when you never did before.

One morning, just as I'd started my shift, I got called into the administrator's office, and when I walked through that door, he was standing shoulder to shoulder with the director of medicine. She says to me, says, "Everyone has noticed your behavioral changes, and we're very concerned for you. Lonnie, nobody even recognizes you anymore." I knew what it was all about, it didn't take a genius to figure it out. They called my bullshit when I gave the excuse that I'd been overworked, so I told them, "Yeah, well, all of us here are high." Next thing I knew, they put me on leave, sent me to a thirty-day program. It didn't do much of shit for me. When I got out, I put myself around other recovering addicts, moved them into my duplex. I led meetings in my living room and went to them beat up on heroin. Hell of a guy, huh?

I did that for a few weeks, leading meetings high, until some recovering doctor friends of mine found me naked behind a neighbor's house, at a clockless hour of the night, laying in a plastic playhouse, with a needle hanging out of my wrist. I had no idea how I got there, or that I was out cold. Or that I had overdosed and died. But there I was, cashing in my chips to the Devil. But he wasn't done with me yet. Not even close.

Those very friends delivered me through the pneumatic doors of the emergency room, where I was brought back from the grave inside the same hospital where all this began. After I recovered, the medical director came into the room and informed me that I'd been let go. That was when things really took a turn. And a turn they went. I was at a bar—this was in El Paso—I met a guy who sold dope. Asked me If I'd be interested in peddling some of the stuff for him. I said sure, what the hell. Later that night I went with him to this dirty little apartment where they conducted business through a false deadbolt in the door. I saw what he made that night, how easy he made it. Wow man, this guy made double what I made annually at the hospital, in the same amount of time, but without all the headache that came with the territory of being a doctor. Inside of four months I was the biggest dope-dealer in El Paso. I did armed robberies on small time dealers and filling stations all up and down Interstate 10. Married twice at the same time, divorced from both of them a month later. Even made one of them get an abortion ... yeah. Me. But God decided to let the hammer come down on me. It came down so hard it felt as though my eyes had been blown out of their smokey sockets. Justice served me on my doorstep with six .38 caliber service revolvers and several warrants for my arrest. They folded me up and canned me. I am facing a slew of charges. Maybe looking at ten to fifteen years—real time, but for now, I am here in the El Paso County lockup, awaiting trial. Counting my sins. Writing to all of the people I've hurt in my life. In particular, this year. I'm going to plead guilty. I deserve everything they throw at me, James.

I dried up real hard in here. A few times I believed I would die. I think I did die. I did. Twice. Once for real, and now in a metaphorical sense. Before you got shipped out, you asked me if I believed in God. And I told you that I didn't know that perhaps he and I shared similar beliefs. But I'm telling you as I was laying on my cot, drowning in sweat, vomiting, shitting my pants, God was the only force I begged to kill me. Make of that as you may. But I am here, crying while I drag my pen across the page. If you think I'm bullshitting, fine, but I'll tell you to kiss it on the ass while it does. Anyway, James, my life, my experience, is the inscrutable truth.

I live with one foot on the trail of regret and the other on the road of my life's forward journey. But you know what I regret most? What I regret even more than being too doped up to see you on your last leave? There was a young man, a dying young man up at the hospital in Albuquerque. Face so cold, cheeks so sunken. He was very nearly dead, and he trusted me. But I stole his drugs, and he died. I will never forget that, never forgive myself for that, never want to.

I was supposed to save lives.

Most sincerely, your brother-in-progress,
Lonnie

THE DARK WOODS

The passing of a mid-July's night left no trace on the floor of the forest. The spits of rain had gone, and the cool wind through the spruces and evergreens had gone, and now there was only the clamor of crickets and other night-ling insects, myriad and without distinction on the cool mountainous air.

The she-wolf in that predawn dark came down a rockslide, silent and with lethal dexterity, to stalk the young raccoon. It was laboriously threading its way among flaring grass to the course of a swollen creek. The she-wolf had marked it down, yellow eyes narrowed in primordial pursuit. She crept up to the raccoon from where it drank idly at the creek edge, phantom-like on crouched legs, her belly hugging the ground. She slunk around the bole of a tree like taffy. She leapt after it, swift and deft as a serpent's strike, her canine grin shone milkblue in the moonlight. In a single graceful motion, the she-wolf hooked her claws into the raccoon's ribs, cocked her skull and sank her teeth into its neck. It never heard her; never even caught scent of her. The raccoon went limp in her jaw-clasp. The she-wolf rose and went on, the little skull of the raccoon lolling with her progress.

In the first grainy wash of light, the she-wolf came out onto a high meadow in a valley in the mountains. She began to waller down in the shelter of a windfall trunk for rest from her hunt. She paused suddenly, as if something had caught her attention, rising now cautiously to nudge her bloody nose about the air. Her ears lay back on her head. She had seen him before he had. The first shot from the rifle thocked in the mud by her forepaws. Tall spray of grass and clots of dirt. Now she was in desperate motion.

The hunter was laying prone upon loose shale and weeds, the forearm of his rifle propped on his wrist. He dug the rifle stock into his shoulder, sighted in, jacked the crosshairs frantically up the back of the animal fleeing broadside to him, and fired. The bullet cracked and rolled across the valley, sounding back in attenuating reiteration. She dropped in an anguished squall, kicked her hind legs about, scrabbled up, was making off again. "Shit," the hunter said. It was a high shot, he knew that. But one thing he knew for certain: there would be blood. He glassed down the meadow with his binoculars, saw dark fingers of blood plastered down the fur of her hindquarters. He watched her go out of sight, dissolving into the woods. The meadow stood windless and silent and slightly coruscant with dew. He climbed to his knees and picked up the rifle, ejected the spent casing and closed the bolt. Then he rose to his feet and slipped the rifle over his shoulder and set out from his position after her.

He located blood tracks dotted erratically among spruce bark and thatchings of pine needles or pine cones and tracked them until he altogether lost sign of the wounded animal. He turned and went up a long slope of second growth spruce and aspens and followed the crest of the ridge northeast to an overlook above the rolling series of ridges. Twenty miles away the bald summit of the Sierra Blanca range shining under the clouds in the ribboned light of the sun. He swept across the folds of valleys with the binoculars for some sign of her. Somewhere down there, she had simply vanished. He scanned the country very slowly. Just downhill from a gaunt service road sat a pickup truck. Slightly obscured by trees. The front of it made a V around the trunk of a canted spruce. He squatted and propped his elbows on his knees and adjusted the focus. The truck was a late thirties or early forties Chevy half-ton pickup. He thought he could see someone inside. Some pinecones, bits of broken glass on the accordioned hood. Nothing moved. He glassed up to the road. It looked like soiled wash gathered there. Then he realized without question that it was absolutely a body. He lowered the binoculars. It was quiet. Not even a bird flew. He glanced up at the sky to measure the progress of the sun. If he hiked out to the wreck, it would be late evening before he got back to his truck, to home. He didn't want to worry his wife, worry the child incubating inside her. But then, he thought, wouldn't you want someone to come save your skinny ass?

At the end of the overlook was a steep slope, a game trail winding down it. Stones scuted with lichens like some curious uranic fur; some in whose faces bore fossils Mesozoic in aspect. He hiked along, his back already wet through with sweat. It was a good hard climb to the wrecked truck, stopping from time to time to get his breath and to mop sweat from his forehead with a kerchief. It was close to noon by the time he got there.

When he approached the pickup, he heard a veritable drone of flies. He hallooed and waited. The air smelled awful. He held the kerchief to his mouth and nose, went forward and opened the driver door. Behind the wheel sat a man dead, his head fallen back, mouth agape. His eyes were open, crescents of matter like cured grout in the cups of them. He looked like he was studying the ceiling with great surprise. Blood dried to black everywhere. A small caliber revolver lay in his palsied grip beside him. A fly danced up his cheek, walked a circle across an eyeball. The hunter shut the door and stepped back. He looked up the slope to where the service road was. He stood there for a long time. He looked back at the truck. Flies, so many of them. It could have happened last night. It could have even happened two days ago.

Walking along the road with his thumb hooked through the shoulder strap of the rifle, he could see the body from which he'd spotted at the overlook. As he drew closer, he saw two black pumps. It was a woman lying face down. She had been shot too. He stood in the road with the sun boiling the nape of his neck. Then he heard it: a wail not much louder than a kitten. He went up to the woman and squat down on one knee, stood the rifle in the gravel. He eased her over onto her side. Black hair all down her face, blankets in her arms. Small writhing movements within. He scanned the landscape. He fished the blankets open with one hand. A newborn. Skin red and mottled and its little legs pedaling weakly, squalling red-gummed at its beleaguered nativity. He stood up then, numb and afflicted. His eyes whited. The rack of his breast plate rising and falling, rising and falling rapidly. He swallowed hard. Then he scooped it up in the bloody blankets. He could feel it moving against his breast. He hushed it and said that it would be okay, that it was safe. That it would remain so, and that he wouldn't let anything happen to it. They had to have come from some place. Maybe there's a house down the road. Maybe in that house, a phone. He took his bearings by the sun and set off back along the road, and so into the direction from which they had come ...

... From time to time stopping to speak to and console the child. He sat on a boulder off the road and spoke to the child about his life. But that did not seem to abate its lamentations.

After a while he sang to it.

By dusk, the cries had paled and paled. And after a while the child quit making any noise altogether, and it died in his arms. He let go the rifle and crashed to his knees, clutching the little child tightly to his chest, holding what cannot be held. The pieces shattered and out of which could not be righted nor made whole again. He sat in the earth, looking down at the child in his arms. The little glassy eyes gave back to him a story that would not be told. He pulled the lids down with his thumb. He held a tiny hand and closed his own eyes. What flesh and blood are made of but can themselves not be forged on any anvil nor shaped upon the mason's stone in all the world's turnings, yet it can be lost between the fingers like a finely seething dust. Just like that. And we may well discover that those for whom death had decreed premature be forever consigned to your heart much like a terminal disease, much like a wound of war. And we shall never forget it.

Night. Dark fell like a shroud, black and formless to the world, such as to its origins. He hadn't seen any sign of civilization. It had begun to rain, and rained hard it did, now falling sheetwise and cutting channels along the shouldering slopes, running irate as an arterial wound. By now he was simply lost. But he slogged on. A half mile further, he could see the lights of a crude church standing in a yellow nimbus among the pines—the light bisected by trees, forming two slurred coronas, like the parthenogenesis of light itself. He went toward it.

The church was composed wholly of mud and shingled up in roofing tin. Sagging windows. There was an addition off in the back, but it was hard spying. He stood in the high grass for a long time looking the place over. Pools of water building in the dooryard there. But when he'd turned to go, light opened out upon him and a voice hailed him from the doorway, inquisitive. He looked. There a figure stood, limned by the interior, lantern oscillating before him, light playing out across the rainy darkness. The voice called to him first in Spanish and then in English, and waved him in.

The place was dimly lit with tallow torch light. Galvanized buckets about the clay floor to catch the leaks through the mud and kindling-wood latilla ceiling. He let the door clap shut behind him. There were isles of pews vacated of any follower. At the altar, a few candles of various sizes burned, and in that runagate light knelt an old woman bent at prayer. A dim oil lamp burned at her side. "Tenemos visita," the old man called to her. The woman rose stiffly and turned to face the man. Her face worn hard as leather, two ropes of slack skin running down her throat to her bosom. "Qué tiene ahí, en sus brazos?" She asked the old man, her fist to her mouth.

"A baby," the hunter interjected.

"A baby?" said the old man, squinting hard at the dark shape nestled within the coat.

"Yes."

"Qué dijo?" the woman asked the old man.

"Dijo que un bebé," he told her.

"Dios mío," she said. "Está vivo?"

The hunter shook his head grimly that it was not alive. The woman gasped, held a fragile palm to her mouth. Their Rorschach shadows swinging across the far wall.

"What were you doing when you found the baby?" the old man wanted to know.

"I was hunting"

"You were hunting."

"Yes."

"I see. Come. Come. Follow me." He looked at the woman. "Haznos café, por favor. Necesito hablar con este hombre."

The woman said okay, and then went away into a small room. The old man went behind her, ducking through the coffin sized doorway, saying for the hunter to again follow.

The room was composed of limestone entire. The windows draped in elk hide. There sat against the south wall a soapstone stove with the stovepipe running through a crude hole in the wall that had been hacked with a pick to quit the room of smoke. Upon the stove where the old woman now set about percolating coffee, were cairns of crockery and pans blackened with cook. A table and two chairs stood before it. A small cot with ticking in the corner. The room smelled very good. Earthy redolence of juniper. Smells of herbs, of dried meat. A tinge of caustic. The old man set the oil lamp on the varnished table of some old wood, nothing more than a refectory table, and eased himself into one of the tall-backed chairs. "Sit," he told the hunter.

"What do you want me to do with the baby?"

"Sit with it."

The hunter sunk into the chair, the child cradled, the blanket dripping and pooling water blackly upon the floor. The old man sat sideways to the table and crossed his legs in a manner the elderly favor. It was quiet a long time. Their faces in that globe of orange lantern light like vapid jack o'lanterns. The old man watched the woman until she turned and nodded her head and went out, closing the door behind her.

"I am a Mennonite," he said. "Or was—I was born Mennonite. They came to Chihuahua, Mexico during the early twenties. From Manitoba, Canada. Myself included. I was a Mennonite, and then converted to Catholicism. I don't know what I am now. I suppose now I am just me."

"And what is it that you do here?"

"I take care of this place with my wife."

"You live here?"

"Yes."

"For how long?"

The old man chuckled. "For long enough. Probably I'd say ten years, going on." He reached into his shirt pocket and produced a pack of readymade cigarettes and held it out toward the hunter.

"Thanks. I gave it up."

The old man nodded and shook one out and tapped the end of it on the table and stuck it between his lips. Then he fished out a lighter from the same pocket and lit it and dropped it back into his shirt pocket again. "Tell me about this child," he said, gesturing with his chin. "Is it yours?"

"No. He ain't mine."

"You found him."

"Yes."

"Where did you find him at?"

"Out on this utility road. I was tracking this wolf I'd shot. I hiked up this mountain and glassed the terrain below and seen a wreck down there just off the side of the road. So I made my way up to it. But it wasn't no wreck. Somethin had gone bad. Real bad. And there he was, this little baby, layin with his mother in the middle of the road, curled up in this blanket."

The old man smoked thoughtfully, very thoughtfully. "You said what you'd come upon was bad. But it was not a wreck."

"No."

"What was it?"

"Something gone wrong. I don't know. But the boy's mother and father had been killed. Shot. I think the father killed the mother and then turned the gun on hisself."

"Did you locate any authorities?"

"I'd gotten lost. You're the first soul I've seen."

"Was the baby alive when you found him?"

"Yes. But he died not very long after."

"I see. Very unfortunate." He folded his arms.

"You said you were tracking a wolf. Those are rather scarce to come by these days. Up here that is. Why were you tracking a wolf?"

"She was killing my calves."

"A she. How could you tell?"

"You could tell by how she did her thing."

"Ah." The old man combed his thin hair with his fingers. "What are your views on God?"

"What about Him?"

"Do you get along with Him?"

"Naw. And I ain't much convinced that He'd get along with me."

"And why is that?"

"Because I've seen far too much meanness in this world to justify his being here."

"Military?"

"Pardon?"

"You were in the Military?"

"I was, yes. 45th Infantry Division. I was there the day we liberated Dachau."

"Dachau? I believe I'd fairly recently read about that in the papers. Refresh my memory. What was Dachau?"

"A concentration camp. A terrible, awful place. I looked for God all over that place. I wanted to find him and wring his neck for what he allowed to happen to those poor people. To the children. I looked for him today too. And guess what. I couldn't even smell him."

The old man drummed his fingers on the table. A smile beginning in the folds of loose skin, this curious hierophant. He said to suggest such a thing as to see through the eyes of God, you would then cease to see anything at all. He said that God is indistinguishable from the white noise and that if God were to separate himself from that, then in turn it would make him an integer of something separate from all else; that ultimately it would render him void from the matrix of humanity. He said for then there would be no judgement, and without judgement, the world is aught it knows to do with itself; hell would be vacated, and every thrall would be here. Among us. He said it is not that the cries of God's creations fall upon deaf ears, but rather that within all the complexities of the universe—through its genesis and unto its ultimate destruction—that God tends to creation with an inscrutable purpose. Lastly, he said that we could never understand God's ways fully, and that if we could, would we not then cease to be mortal? The old man stubbed out the cigarette on a china plate on the table and rose from the chair stiffly and gimped to the stove.

"What brought you here?" said the hunter.
"To New Mexico."

"I came here as a refugee," the old man said. He got two clay cups down from a cupboard. "By a means of escape from my former life." He poured coffee into the cups and brought them to the table. The old man pushed one of the cups to the hunter and sat and crossed his legs.

"What were you running from?"

The old man sipped the coffee. "I was on the run because of atrocity. Because of destruction."

"The Revolution?"

"Yes. Many will tell you that it was over. But it was not over for a long time." The old man studied the ceiling intently. Perhaps as if his thoughts were there. "I had come to be indignant of God. I believed him to be wrathful. So I sought out evidence of his kindness, of his benevolence in this world."

"Did you ever find it? The evidence."

"I found that man had not seriously considered the marvel of atrocity. God and the Devil are at war and the war front is man's pulsebeat. Do you see? Darkness is part of the world and for everything necessary to it. That is what I found."

The hunter looked down at the child in the lantern light. Delicate face in eternal sleep. Then he looked up at the old man. The old man said, "It is simple to see that naught save that of great sorrow could drive man to have woeful views of God. But sorrow without belief is a fool's sorrow. Drink your coffee."

The hunter drank. After a while, he said, "How do I get to a hospital from here? Maybe they can find out who this boy is and bury him proper."

The old man cleared his throat and rose up out of the chair. "I will take him," he said, swiping the seat of his pants with his hands. "We will take him outside, at this moment. To my truck. I will drive him to the hospital and report the crime scene. Could you navigate to where his parents are?"

"Yes. But not from here. I could take you, take you or whoever I need to, from the base of the mountain."

"Is that where you are parked?"

"Yes. The cattle guard off West Side road."

"I will meet you there tomorrow. We will get there early. Early as, in six o'clock, and we will lead the authorities there. We will source out the location. Everything will be all right."

"I hope you're right."

The old man took up the lantern and adjusted the wick. "Okay. Vamos a mi troca."

Crossing through the nave the old woman took the hunter by his hand. "My husband is curandero. Some says he is. You know what is curandero?"

"Yes ma'am. I do."

The old woman stared fixedly into his eyes. He saw worlds, universes.

"Vaya con Dios," she said.

They were going in the rain, the two of them, the old man leading the way with the lantern in one hand and cradling the child in the other. The man followed close behind, his shoulders pulled up for the rain. By a pine-board smokehouse sat the old man's truck. The old man called out over the ripping rain for the hunter to open the door. He did. He overtook the old man, opened the door whining on its livid hinges, like a rusty wing, and watched the old man carefully place the child on the center of the bench seat. The old man pushed the blanket away from the child's face and said a quick blessing. A jagged chain of lightning, blue as cobalt, listed across the sky and delivered the hunter a simian's first chasmic vision of the world, and—occurring almost instantaneously and back to dark again—a final view of the porcelain face that he took for some cognate of his heart's ultimate dread.

  The old man got in and fired up the truck. "Get in," he said. "You aren't going to walk in this. I won't allow it."

  "I wouldn't know how to direct you, sir."

  "There's only one road up this way, you know. You came from the west. I watched you.
Now get in before you drown in this mess."

  When they got to his truck by the cattle guard in the foothills, the rain had stopped and now there was only lightning pulsating in electric relay, distant, silent. A small milky moon hung between darker folds of cloud like a hole in the sky. He thanked the old man and opened the door, but the old man stopped him. "Let me ask you something," he said. "Before you go."

  "Okay."

  "Where do you think one might hear the voice of God?"

  "Tell me."

  "The voice of God speaks in highest volume through such things that do not speak at all."

  The man speculated him to mean trees or stones—things like that—but the old man, studying, said, "When that voice stops, only then will you realize that you've been hearing it the whole of your life. And sometimes," he said. "It's the most unlikely of creatures from which he speaks."

  The hunter nodded, thanked him again and climbed out into the road. He turned and lifted a hand farewell. He couldn't see whether the old man had done the same or not. He watched the old man swing the truck around, the atavistic vehicle chugging, clots of blue smoke coughing from the pipe, and very soon the truck was altogether lost among the dark woods. The man walked to his truck and stuck his key in the door, unlocked it, and climbed under the steering wheel. He just sat there. He couldn't put a name to the feeling. It was sorrow, but it was something else. Something he'd felt many times in a country far from this one. He blew air out of his cheeks and drummed his fingers on the steering wheel and looked at the night into which the old man had returned. Then he started the truck.

When he got back to the house, he parked and walked up the porch steps and into the house to the kitchen. He dropped the keys on the counter. Beside the keys lay a 45th infantry division zippo lighter. He lifted the zippo from the countertop and ran his thumb across the face of it. "Thunderbird," he muttered. He adjusted the rifle on his shoulder and turned and crossed through the roseate glow from the hearth in the living room and stopped short of the bedroom door. A platinum band of candlelight underneath of it.

He eased the bedroom door open. His wife was sitting in the bed, leaned against the iron headboard reading a book. He went on in slowly and gave a conflicted smile.

"Thought you done took off on me," she said.

"That was the plan," said the hunter, lowering himself down onto the edge of the bed. His wife marked a spot on the page with her finger and closed the book over it, and said, "You were gone a awful long time. Did you get that wolf?"

"No."

"That doggone thing. We can talk to that old boy out by Three Rivers. The one you said you was going to talk to."

"Yeah."

"Well. You look starved. They's food on the warmer."

"I ain't hungry."

"What's the matter? You've got that look on your face."

The hunter looked about at the dusty slat-board floor, elbows on the thin worn knees of his britches. Wind moaned on the roof.

"Darling," she said, reaching a hand onto his lap. "You can talk to me. You can talk to me about anything in the world. What happened?"

"I ain't real sure I'd know how to tell it."

"The beginning is where I'd start. Sorry."

"I'm goin to be out early tomorrow."

"Where are you going?"

"Out. Got to handle some things."

"They's something that you ain't telling me."

"I told it all to you."

"Fine. I guess it's just best I ought not know."

"That sounds good."

"Please tell me what's the matter, would you?"

He opened his palm, mud dried to dust falling from the lines. "Well. You ever have dreams, and when you wake up, you ain't sure that you know what they mean? And then maybe something happens later on, and you're liable to make sense of it?"

"I don't think I'm following, sweetheart. So you had some dreams last night?"

"Well, a dream—I know it, you're fixin to think I'm crazy."

"I already done thought you was crazy."

"I'm bein serious."

"All right. I'll be courteous, I promise. So tell me about this dream."

The hunter looked at the ceiling as if across which were writ meaning, substance. "It was strange, not much to it," he said. "Anyways, I was in country I'd never been, country all flat-like; each direction I looked there was nothin. Just grass as far as I could see. I was lost out there and I knew I couldn't turn back because ain't nothin that was there. I was afraid because the sun was goin dark, and it was very cold." He paused. "Then I saw the sun comin up again, and it was growin bigger. Then I seen all this life comin up from the horizon; cattle, horses, birds, all runnin or flyin toward me wild-eyed and terrified. And then I realized that it wasn't no sun risin. It was a prairie fire. And I was standin there tremblin, afraid to the bone. And you would think you would turn and run away with the animals, but somethin told me to walk toward it, to the fire. And only when I made that first step, did I lose my fear. I wasn't afraid no more, I think, because I knew that when I got there, that I would be warm."

In the night, he dreamt no dreams and slept poorly and awoke sometime during those hours in which no two hands intersect, and lay staring at the ceiling in the dark. He thought about the child in the road. The mother. The father. The cries, oh God, the cries. How long had you been laying there in all that heat, crying into the cold flesh that bore you into this world, this world that would not have you? It was quiet in the house, quiet outside. And it was guilt that he couldn't route from his heart. And it would not be until the night of his death that he would wield the child with him, abridging the ultimate dark, with the light of a hundred suns. He climbed out of the bed and ambled into the kitchen and fetched a jar of milk from the icebox and stood drinking. He looked out the kitchen window upon that sleep-drawn darkland. A lone tractor truck and trailer laboring along the highway two miles distant. Far off, the gypsum sea in its ancient spread. And occurring just then in that pseudo dawn, the rim of the desert seemed to rise up into the well of firmament, clearing away the constellations like a demonic lycoperdon, making a violet day out of the desert nightcountry, whereafter no bird flew and man stood trembling, not at God, but at man unto himself in its afterimage for a millennia to come.

Acknowledgements

The author would like to thank his editor, Patrick Trotti, for his fine work, insightful eye, skill, and patience. He would also like to thank his wife, Alexandria; his mother, Lori Whitley; his father, Todd Whitley; his brother, Zachary Goza; his mother- and father-in-law, Amanda and Oscar Veyna; and everyone else for their encouragement and support along the way. Finally, he would like to thank Scott Phillips and Anthony Neil Smith for their mentorship and friendship.

Donovan Whitley was born in Ardmore, Oklahoma and raised in Wichita, Kansas. He currently lives in southern New Mexico. *Wickedness and Folly* is his first book.

www.ingramcontent.com/pod-product-compliance
Lightning Source LLC
LaVergne TN
LVHW041611070526
838199LV00052B/3083